The
Palace
of Tears

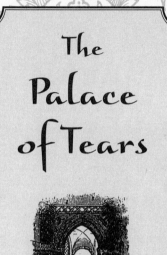

Alev Lytle Croutier

DELTA TRADE PAPERBACKS

A Delta Book
Published by
Dell Publishing
a division of
Random House, Inc.
1540 Broadway
New York, New York 10036

Copyright © 2000 by Alev Lytle Croutier
Map by Jeffrey L. Ward
Cover painting: "In the Harem" by
Jean Jules Lecomte de Nouy (1842–1923),
The Fine Art Society, London, UK/Bridgeman Art Library
Cover design by Marietta Anastassatos

Delta® is a registered trademark of
Random House, Inc., and the colophon is
a trademark of Random House, Inc.

ISBN: 0-385-33491-5

Book design by Virginia Norey

Reprinted by arrangement with Delacorte Press
Manufactured in the United States of America
Published simultaneously in Canada

January 2002

BVG 10 9 8 7 6 5 4 3 2 1

For Angelica,
the enigmatist
the dearest friend

This is a work of fiction. Not only the
characters and events but also the historical facts
have been sacrificed to tell the story.
Do not believe a word of it.

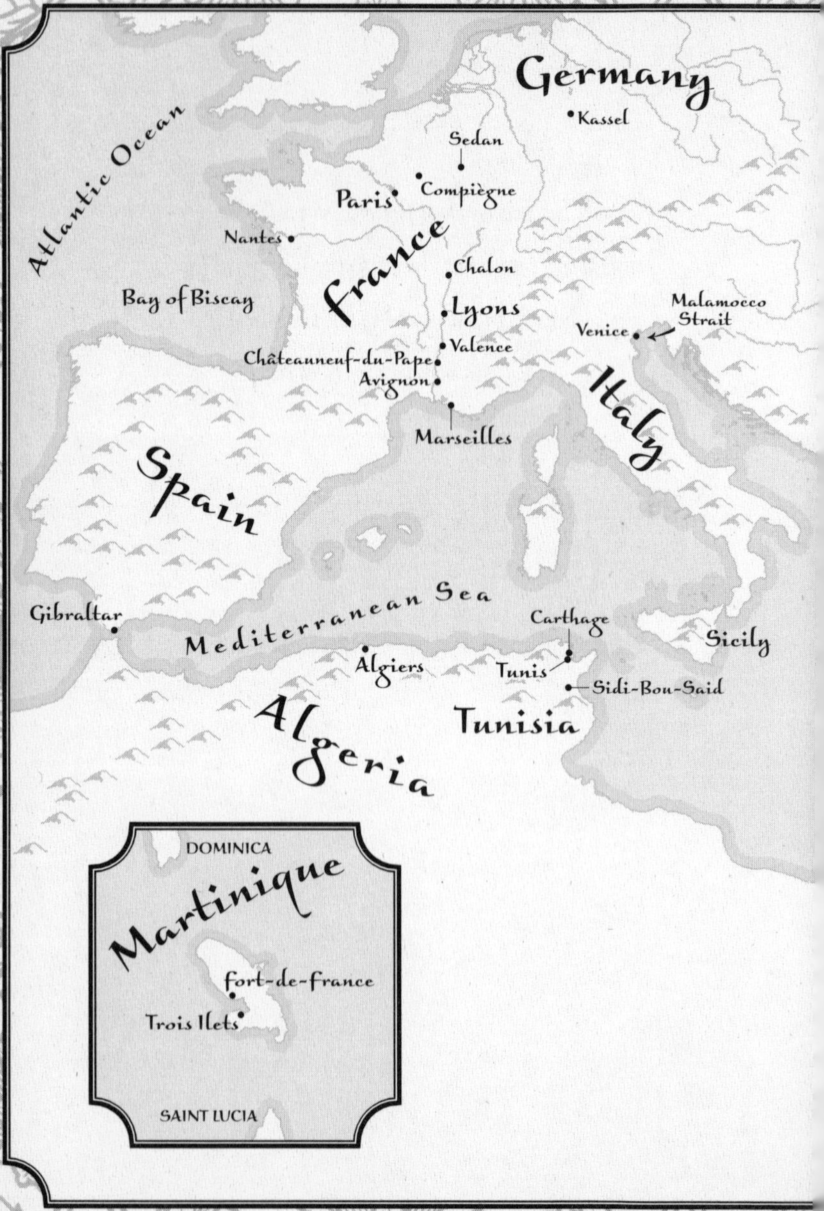
Germany
Kassel
Sedan
Compiègne
Paris
Atlantic Ocean
Nantes
France
Chalon
Bay of Biscay
Lyons
Malamocco
Strait
Venice
Valence
Châteauneuf-du-Pape
Avignon
Italy
Marseilles
Spain
Mediterranean Sea
Gibraltar
Carthage
Sicily
Algiers
Tunis
Sidi-Bou-Said
Algeria
Tunisia
DOMINICA
Martinique
Fort-de-France
Trois Ilets
SAINT LUCIA

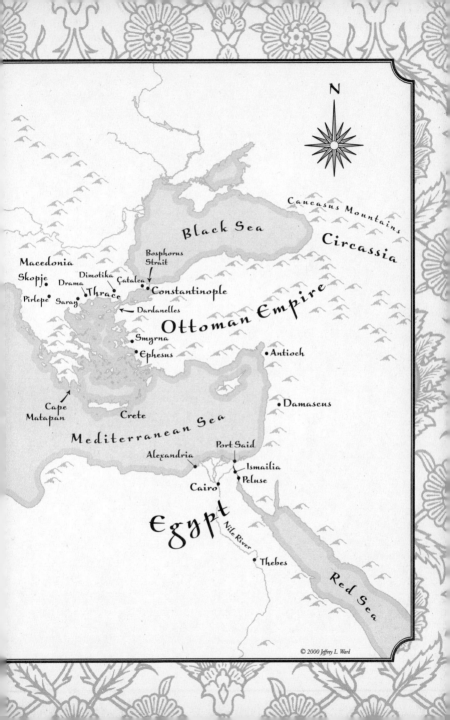

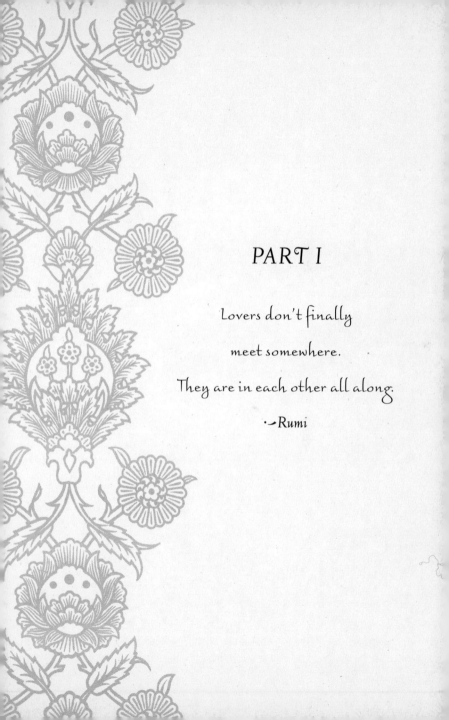

PART I

Lovers don't finally

meet somewhere.

They are in each other all along.

—Rumi

1

His family wanted him to live in the country and cultivate grapes as the rest of them had for twenty generations, but Casimir de Châteauneuf had finer needs.

Casimir was a dreamer. He wanted to find his destiny
before his destiny could find him.

The year was 1868. Europe was in a frenzy, seeking
its spiritual opposite in the recesses of the Maghreb and
the Levant. An obsession for Orientalism permeated
everything, from pulp fiction and fashion to the grand
canvases of Delacroix.

But what intrigued everyone the most was that, after
years of toil, the waters of the Mediterranean and the
Indian Ocean were about to merge in the Suez, a symbolic union of the East and the West, a union promising
faster trade and immense fecundity.

Casimir de Châteauneuf was thirty-five.

He had already succeeded in turning grapes into gold.

~~·~~

Casimir's childhood was monotonously vast vineyards. His adolescence, dark cellars. The estate was called Grange du Souvenir. The town was called Châteauneuf-du-Pape.

His wife was called Espérance. And his children were named André, Antoine, and Alphonse.

Casimir knew every street, every house, every person in Châteauneuf-du-Pape. He had pursued all the vices that prevailed in the provinces.

"I'm bored—bored to death. Bored as never before," he confided to a friend.

He set off for Paris to market the wine and to explore the city's unique perversions.

His great talent for assimilation and his country gentleman's social ease quickly gained him entrance to the best men's clubs and women's salons. With dismissive panache, he grasped the nuances of *couture*. Refining his accent in no time, he cultivated his eloquence.

He kept a mistress, an alluring courtesan, who lived above the arcades at the Palais Royal. What distinguished her was an abundant red mane and small, voluptuous lips. (In fact, important men whispered to each other about her "other" small, voluptuous lips which compensated sweetly for their own deficiencies.)

Casimir could see the turrets of the Louvre out of her bedroom window. He could measure the pulse of commerce parading through rue de Rivoli. He could spend hours at the Bibliothèque Nationale, engrossed in unusual books and journals, in pursuit of things that had occurred during his boyhood in the country. He could gush through the volumes written, the continents explored, the machines invented.

Casimir celebrated follies of luxury and every new expression of the arts. In the evenings, the theater and the opera. Three times a week, fencing and pistols at the Cartoucherie. On Tuesdays, Bezique with foreign businessmen at the Faubourg Saint-Honoré.

Every Tuesday afternoon at four, a retinue of street people bared their palms outside the club. Among them, he distributed the day's revenue.

2

On that fated day, Casimir de Châteauneuf was returning to his mistress's after a Bezique game. He found himself wedged among spectators on rue de Rivoli, watching
a cortège of fancy carriages enter the courtyard of the
Tuileries Palace. From these carriages descended gentlemen in knee breeches and silk stockings. They held out
their arms to the ladies, ladies dressed in billowing crinolines, breasts almost bare except where concealed beneath
jewelry and furs. They strolled under a marquée into the
Pavilion de l'Horloge, where Swiss Guards with plumed
helmets stood to attention. Then they disappeared out
of sight.

For Casimir de Châteauneuf, the spectacle was a scene
straight from grand theater, where a solid yet translucent
curtain separated the performers from the audience. It

gave him an odd feeling as if separate realities were merging, a sense that had the quality of a premonition.

He wondered if he was meant to cross the line.

He stopped at 220 rue de Rivoli at A. Webb's, the famous wine and brandy dealer. Over cigars and special reserve Châteauneuf-du-Pape—Casimir's gift—he and Webb negotiated an arrangement advantageous to both.

How effortless things had become. A good smoke, a glass of wine. He walked out of A. Webb's smiling, filled with a sense of overflowing gratitude for the miracle of existence.

It was autumn. Gold and copper leaves through the park were almost knee deep. Like grapes at harvest but feathery light.

Casimir de Châteauneuf felt himself the happiest man in the world as he wandered idly through a maze of streets and corners, courtyards and shortcuts in this city of false perspectives and perfect symmetry.

He circled the Place Vendôme, walked fast down rue Saint Honoré, past the Comédie Française, then took a final shortcut at the Montpensier gallery, cutting through the dark alley to the gardens where little children played ring-around-the-rosy.

Under the hollow arcades of the Palais Royal, golden light filtered through the arches. He stopped to get some snuff, circled the square, pausing to gaze at the windows of medal shops, and to buy antique tin soldiers for

André, Antoine, and Alphonse. And a satin bustier with silk rosettes for Espérance—the kind in vogue among Parisian women that season, the kind that lifted their busts nearly up to their necks—certain that her modesty would never allow her to indulge. Even in private.

He was distracted by a shop window with no display except a black velvet curtain on which was painted one word: *Orientalia*.

It had such an erotic ring to it that Casimir was disturbed by a fluttering of his heart. After rolling the word *Orientalia* round his mouth as if it were a piece of freshly plucked fig, he entered the shop.

A somber space, strongly pungent smell of untanned leather mingled inside with attar of roses. It was cluttered with typical *bric-à-brac* from the Orient—the hookah, the turban, the dagger, the tambourine—but selected with a keen eye.

In a smaller annex was a collection of fine miniature portraits, oil replicas of actual people's faces, with the most intricate detail. Despite their small size, the lingering expression etched on each face hinted at stories that longed to be told.

But of all the portraits, the face of a young woman hypnotized him. No matter from which angle Casimir viewed the portrait, her eyes remained locked with his as if following the movement of his eyes. He experienced a peculiar sensation as though the painting were alive.

She was dressed in a green caftan with flowing sleeves, embroidered with golden tulips. It was difficult to guess the color of her hair, as it was concealed under a jeweled turban, but her skin was like ivory.

Her eyes: one blue, the other yellow.

The face was terrifyingly familiar yet his memory could not place it anywhere. The edge of the gilded frame was inscribed with the words *La Poupée*. The doll.

"Who is she?" he asked.

The owner of the shop did not know. A painter who had traveled to the Orient, a very short young man who called himself Nomad, had sold it to him.

"Where can I find him?" asked Casimir de Châteauneuf. After all, the Orient was vast, encompassing all the lands of Islam along the Mediterranean.

The man shrugged his shoulders. "He's a painter. Here today, gone tomorrow. I have no way of knowing, but you may want to pursue the vendors in Montmartre."

Casimir de Châteauneuf bought the miniature for a price. In its green velvet case embroidered with golden tulips, it seemed to contain an invisible life infused with destiny.

3

That night the woman of the miniature entered Casimir de Châteauneuf's dream.

He was wandering in a city of domes and slim minarets where everyone spoke an incomprehensible language. Murmurs spread like locusts through a labyrinth of alleys. She was sitting alone in a courtyard, sobbing, her tears filling an empty fountain. Exotic fruit trees, flowers, and birds surrounded her but she seemed to be in some sort of prison. Her accent was flavored, cinnamony, like that of a slave girl but her countenance radiated the elegance of a princess. *Je vous aime. Je vous aime.* The words escaped her lips like smoke rings, floating far into the dream void. He had heard her voice before in his dreams. Their eyes met. He was seized by an intense longing to be near her. He reached out to touch her.

With a start, he sat up in bed, staring at the moonlit wall. Furtive footsteps puttered on the roof. A screech. Only a yawling cat in heat, but the image of the girl was irretrievable, when his consciousness congealed.

All night long, unable to return to the dream, Casimir made love to his mistress, with a lightness that exhaled from his whole being, not only the lower and narrow part of his body. He sensed for the first time that it was neither the intensity of the carnal urge nor the familiar repertoire of undulations that love was made of, but the surrender to the ebb and flow of the lovers' communal breath. Together, they abandoned their bodies and rode an invisible magic carpet through the clouds above the pollarded trees of the Palais Royal (as in the painting of "The Dream" by Puvis de Chavannes, she would describe years later). The rising sun tinted their vulnerable forms. The sky was a splash of saffron red. The trees, all clipped into the same shape, extending infinitely like a paisley sea of leaves.

Casimir left his mistress on her bed, undone, infused with a sacred glow she had not previously known. She craved to hold on to it and to the man who could accompany her through those rapturous swells.

His sudden abandonment, she would never forgive.

4

With superhuman intensity, Casimir climbed all the way up to Montmartre, the hotbed of artistic ferment. He asked for a painter who had journeyed to the East.

"But there are so many of them these days, Monsieur. It's the fashion. How else can a young man escape from this bourgeois morality, this prosaic realism of the metropolis? How else can he free himself from the sexual repression of this Christian monogamy?"

"You may want to try Monsieur Gérôme's studio down near Saint Georges," another suggested.

Casimir cleaved his way through a street demonstration of communards, to the studio of the most famous Orientalist painter. Inside, the carpenters were building a roof terrace replete with fountains and palm trees. A group of art students were gathered around a model, arranging her in the pose of a reclining odalisque. She was dressed in a caftan embroidered with tulips, similar to the one the girl in the miniature wore. It was as if he had entered a scene from *One Thousand and One Nights*.

He asked where the robe had come from. No one knew.

He begged the model to sell him the caftan, even proceeding to disrobe her. Although he was aware of the ridiculousness of his actions, he could not bring himself to care.

The model wept.

The students threw him out on the street.

Along the picturesque yet insalubrious quarters of narrow and crooked roads, he asked each vendor, each landlord about a painter named Nomad. No one seemed to know until a blind ragpicker with a crushed top hat reached for Casimir and said, "Oh, him, the dwarf. He's gone back to the Orient."

Later that day, Casimir de Châteauneuf set off for "the Orient."

5

The Orient was where the sun rose.

Casimir de Châteauneuf began the long journey from Paris to Marseilles, France's gateway to the Orient. First, he took the stagecoach, then the steamer from Chalon to Lyons, catching the Rhône boat as far as Valence, where a ghostly thick fog delayed them. Then the post chaise to Avignon as he had always done on his return from Paris to Châteauneuf-du-Pape.

But this time he did not stop at Grange du Souvenir to see his family. His thoughts, driven only by the single-mindedness of a greater desire, did not even include them. They would be content to receive his gifts. They would not even know of his departure. They would eventually forget him.

From Avignon, he rode the train to Marseilles, where

he boarded *La Sirène*, a steam packet of two hundred horsepowers, which ambled like a drunkard.

Casimir stood for a long time, draped in his pelisse like Childe Harold, leaning against the rail and gazing at the coast of Provence as it gradually vanished into the fog, utterly lost in the reverie of the young woman in the miniature with one blue eye, and the other yellow.

6

After twelve days of wild winds and heavy waves, of rolling and pitching, Casimir de Châteauneuf, perched up in the bow, spyglass in hand, sighted the Egyptian shores. His first impression of the Orient was of a shimmering light that bounced like quicksilver on the water.

He disembarked *La Sirène* in Alexandria, eyes wide open, gulping down a bellyful of bright colors. Never had he seen such a menagerie of deliciously villainous faces that grinned, glowered, and suggested every peculiarity.

Among this everlasting succession of ruffians, he searched for a painter named Nomad, clawing his way through a long range of bazaars, swarms of flies, and yelping dogs, through half-naked, sore-eyed Arabs who held the dread of the plague.

Yet he had no luck.

He left for Cairo, where he boarded an English boat, gliding the Nile upstream toward Thebes. Fresh eggs for breakfast and plum pudding at Christmas. In the mornings, he shot crocodiles and in the afternoons, he took tea.

As they descended the second cataract, he recalled Flaubert's exclamation while he slid down the same: "I've got it! Eureka! Her name is Emma Bovary."

He, too, wished for a revelation. His eyes followed the North Star.

He rode a camel over a mighty sepulchre of a ruined city where at every turn a telltale monument stared at him from its grave. A shattered visage, broken columns, crumbling walls, fragments of granite and marble thrust themselves out of loose earth, as if struggling for resurrection.

> *Nothing beside remains. Round the decay*
> *Of that colossal wreck, boundless and bare,*
> *The lone and level sands stretch far away.*

He rode on burning sands under a burning sun. To one side of him was a yawning chasm, in which hundreds of seminaked Arabs toiled to disentomb the stone body of a pharaoh long buried in the sand. On the other side, another group unveiled a temple as entire as the ancient Egyptians had left it.

At a higher altitude, Casimir was stranded in a flash flood. He witnessed a bubbling yellow torrent rushing down the valley of the riverbed, sweeping along with it a mass of broken statues, trees, and branches. He saw the water swirl and swell around a wooden shack, a river of rapids and whirlpools carrying it off with great force.

Suddenly, a noise like thunder struck and the shack collapsed into the water, sweeping away a screaming man.

When Casimir had the body dug out of the mud, the man was still clutching some paintings but the images had washed off in the muddy waters of the flood. Casimir tried desperately to revive him but no life was left.

He was told that the man's name was Nomad. A dwarf that painted beautiful miniature portraits. In fact, he had painted every person in town.

Casimir asked the rescuers to retrieve something, anything that might have been left of Nomad's shack.

There was nothing but mud.

"To be so close as to almost touch and yet to miss!"

He continued toward Damascus, seeking consolation for a time in erotic and narcotic highs. Still, something persistently beckoned him.

One day on his journey, from out of nowhere, a band of Arab tribesmen brandishing tufted lances galloped alongside, making wild gesticulations. They spared

Casimir's life but grabbed all he had, except the miniature of the girl, which he had concealed in the sand.

Stripped of all, except mirage after mirage of the girl's face, her pellucid voice pealing forth the strobes of a song, *je vous aime, je vous aime,* he wandered. The sweet and amorous note of her lament still echoed with the rapture which seemed to resound across the entire Orient.

He toiled through an infernally rocky terrain that refused to grow anything but stones. He climbed citadels, and fed on cicadas. To every camel herder, every gravedigger, every merchant, he showed the miniature. But no one could tell him who she was. Here women's faces were not seen. Besides, idolatry, which the miniature represented, was against their faith.

"But the eyes," Casimir told them. "Surely you can see the eyes!"

7

Near Antioch, Casimir de Châteauneuf joined a group of the maimed and infirm on a pilgrimage to a sacred spring where an *evliya*, a seer, lived. The pilgrims sensed that Casimir's suffering was as great as theirs, his irises filled with such dark impurities.

The seer, who was said to be two hundred years old, looked at Casimir with eyes so clear that one's soul could drown in them. "You must wait for your kismet to find you," he told the demented and disheveled young man. "You are blocking its light."

"But I've come from so far away."

"Then, you must go back to where you started and stand still."

When a group of British archaeologists rescued

Casimir near Ephesus and brought him to Smyrna, he was suffering from sun fever which caused endless delusions. Through the grace of the French Consul, he was transported back to Marseilles, although almost too fragile to sail.

8

By the time they delivered Casimir de Châteauneuf to Grange du Souvenir, the sense of reality that others agreed on was totally lost to him. He slipped back and forth between twisted chambers of logic. Even in delirium, his eyes remained focused on the point of infinity of a restless dream. The girl with one blue, one yellow eye lured him through a labyrinth of cities similar to the ones on his journey to the Orient. He chased her through corridors, closed doors, and down secret stairways.

She always slipped away.

Until one day, he caught up with her and took her in his arms. Their hearts were beating against each other.

He had hurled himself on the floor, his arms raised in the air as if he were trying to reach someone when

Espérance woke him up with the ampoules, the vials she had come to put on his back to ease his pain.

A tear was rolling down Casimir's cheek.

Espérance took care of him. She had ice brought from the mountains. She made sorbets out of snow. Compresses out of lavender.

She met all the attributes of a good spouse but Espérance had no affinities with Casimir and lacked the slightest hint of sensuality. The bustier, the one he had sent her just before his epic journey to the Orient, she would never wear for fear of vulgarity.

André, Antoine, and Alphonse offered their father frogs and lizards, creatures of cold blood to bring down his burning. The creatures' bulging eyes and limpid souls gave him amusement.

His sons were the reason he had endured the cloying domesticity and monotony of conjugal life. But even paternity proved not to be as strong an emotion as he had anticipated.

By the end of three months, Casimir had lost his fever. Although he no longer stared into that undefinable nothingness, he had also lost his dreams. He had become *comme il faut*, morally wasted and displaying a suffocating lethargy. A languidness made him drag his feet along the ground, as if the strength sufficient to raise them had failed.

He had also lost his desire for worldly things, for Paris

and for the mistress with the red mane and small, voluptuous lips. The friends with whom he had once played Bezique or drunk absinthe. The library, the theater, the opera. The ladies with billowing crinolines promenading along the Tuileries.

He had changed. Life was no longer an experience but an exercise. Only the presence of death bound him to life. That's what lured him to the hunt, which he pursued with the same obsession with which he had pursued the face in the miniature. The precision of aiming, the sulfurous odor of gunpowder, the quick release of pulling the trigger became his sublimation.

He remained in Châteauneuf-du-Pape and tended the vineyards as the Mistral threatened to tear them down. To protect them from that cold, dry, capricious wind, he had devised an ingenious way of tying the vines.

His family was in ecstasy to see him so engaged, to see that he had once again become one of them. And it pleased them to see Grange du Souvenir thrive so because Casimir attended to everything.

But it would not last long.

9

That autumn, a plague struck the Provence vineyards in the form of *Phylloxera vastatrix*. The vintners watched in horror as the roots of the vines succumbed helplessly to the greed of this tenacious pest. Having already lost their faith in science, which had proved incapable of discovering a cure for the epidemic, they chose to destroy the plants that had for generations provided them with the highest-quality wine. Many resolved to replace the vineyards with olive or chestnut. As the effigies of vines burned in bonfires along the countryside, a malignant ferment filled the air, at once sweet and sickening.

Casimir refused to conform. The only thing that spurred him on now was the continual chain of surmounted difficulties. At no cost would he surrender Grange du Souvenir to such defeat. There had to be a way. What if . . .

10

Casimir de Châteauneuf returned to Paris.

His mistress reclaimed him but he could not make love to her. She tried every craft, every potion, every plaything. After all she was a demimondaine, devoted to the cultivation of the erotic arts.

She would have expelled him from her house but for the memory of their lovemaking the night before his departure to the Orient. She reclined next to him longing to retrieve that instance. Casimir did not touch her. He lay in the dark with eyes burning like a tiger's in the night.

"Don't you love me?" she asked.

"Love is the name given to sorrow only to console those who suffer," he replied. "We suffer because we either desire what we have not or we possess what we no longer desire."

Paris was in black and white and rouge, colors that seemed somber and restrained in their controlled elegance—such a contrast to the regions of the Orient, for which he felt a renewed longing.

Casimir began to dine regularly at the Véfour or the Café Anglais, the haunts of the young aristocracy, rubbing shoulders with the likes of the Duc de Rivoli, Prince Paul Demidoff, the Marquis de Modena. His sphere of acquaintance rippled swiftly, every day insinuating its way closer to the Palace of the Tuileries.

At the Café du Helder Casimir met Ferdinand de Lesseps, who was building the canal through Suez. It was rumored that years of intrigue in London and Paris, Cairo and Constantinople had won him the concession.

Handsome and tenacious, Lesseps charmed everyone with a vividly energetic and theatrical vocabulary. He was impulsive yet reflective.

He was also a cousin of the Empress, Eugénie de Montijo.

It was a wet and gloomy day, Paris suffering from its chronic *grisaille*. The men drank absinthe to warm themselves in cafés.

"Eccentric life could cultivate significant originality, and from this originality would come great and unusual exploits," Lesseps told Casimir de Châteauneuf.

"Aren't such exploits then their own justification?"

"Precisely."

The two men thus formed an acquaintance possible only through a trick of destiny. They gulped down another glass of the "Green Fairy."

"To the Orient, then."

"To the Orient."

11

The idea of linking the Mediterranean and the Red Sea had first occurred during the pharaonic age around 2000 B.C. Necho II had begun constructing a canal in 600 B.C., but it had been abandoned.

In 1798, Napoléon Bonaparte sailed to Egypt on a flagship called *The Orient*. At the risk of his life, he searched for the ruins of this old canal with only two guides accompanying him. During the expedition, he lost one guide and two horses.

The Egyptians later described how each man had carried a loaf of bread spiked on his bayonet and a leather bag of water round his neck and walked as if in a trance through a ghostly mist.

When Bonaparte discovered the remains of the ancient canal near Suez, he was inflamed. But his engineers did not support his enthusiasm since they believed that the level of the Red Sea waters was much higher than the Mediterranean.

Even in exile, Bonaparte copied extracts from a book on the ancient canal, and he wrote, "The piercing of the Isthmus," as a note to himself. "That *is* the key."

For another seventy years no one dared approach the project; the challenge of engineering seemed much too colossal.

12

It would be Ferdinand de Lesseps, who had spent years in Egypt as a diplomat and formed strong alliances, who ultimately possessed the imagination, the will to pursue the Napoléonic vision.

On November 30, 1854, after years of toil and of raising funds, Lesseps signed the agreement with the Egyptian government to build the canal. The concession would last for ninety-nine years.

Lesseps had an almost supernatural confidence in his planning and building skills. But his greatest asset was the ability to gather all the prime players in a grand theater of history to believe in his "moral conviction." Certain that he had a universal obligation to humanity, Lesseps called his enterprise "Compagnie Universelle."

On April 25, 1859, the first pickax blow was struck near Peluse. The digging of the canal continued for ten years. More than 1.5 million Egyptian workers participated, of whom 125,000 lost their lives.

13

Casimir de Châteauneuf drove down rue de Rivoli with Lesseps in the gala Cinderella coach, as the spectators gawked at the cortège entering the courtyard of the Tuileries. He descended from the carriage wearing knee breeches, a dress coat with gold buttons, and silk stockings. He held out his arms for the ladies to descend from their carriages, ladies in billowing crinolines, their breasts almost bare, except where covered with jewelry and furs.

Following the other guests, he passed under a marquée into the Pavilion de l'Horloge where Swiss Guards with plumed helmets stood at attention. They belonged to the same corps as the ones who had given their lives to defend Louis XVI and Marie Antoinette.

Casimir ascended the stately staircase, the guards lined up on both sides like statues, and disappeared into the luxurious domain of the Emperor and the Empress of France.

14

The entire ballroom was lit with hundreds of beeswax candles, everything in shades of white except for the red velvet drapery embroidered with the gold Napoléonic eagles spread over the thrones. Everyone was dressed in white.

In such an atmosphere, Casimir de Châteauneuf found himself waltzing with the Empress Eugénie, who glided like a swan in her white tulle dress trimmed with velvet bows and gold fringe.

"If we can graft the rootstock of the vines afflicted with *Phylloxera* with resistant varieties from the Aegean, we might be able to invent a crossbreed," Casimir told the Empress, as they whirled. "It has never been tried."

The Empress seemed amused by this young man whose eyes were as vacant as hers. As a girl, she had poisoned herself for thwarted passion (she still could taste the phosphorus scraped off matches and dissolved in milk). Since then, having lost her emotional vulnerability, Eugénie could respond to her countless admirers with only indifferent flirtation.

Obviously, Casimir de Châteauneuf too had known and suffered the consequences of love. Obviously, like herself, he had amputated his heart. Why else would a man be so aloof in his self-possession?

15

That autumn Casimir de Châteauneuf was among those who took the train from the Gare du Nord to Compiègne, "the heavenly region where social aspirations promised consummation."

Every fall season this château, where Napoléon Bonaparte and Joséphine had celebrated their honeymoon, turned into the playground of the court. In weeklong segments, each known as a *série*, guests arrived in clusters of a hundred, all in pursuit of a favor, a transaction, an intrigue.

The mannered display of status was the currency of each *série*. The first *série* was for necessary people, the second for bores, the third for the fashionable set, the fourth for the intellectuals.

At the banquet room decorated with rococo angels

and pompous allegorical murals of cupids and bows, Casimir sat between his mistress and Lesseps, who was the guest of honor.

Over dinner, the Empress announced her intention to inaugurate the Suez Canal. "We shall sail to Egypt on the imperial yacht. On the way, we will stop at the city of Constantinople and pay honor to the Sultan, who graced us with his own visit last year."

She smiled recalling how, after a lavish feast at the Élysée, the handsome Sultan had raised the Sèvres finger-bowl, with slices of citrus floating in it, and gulped down the water. How the rest of her court had followed suit in order not to humiliate him.

She asked Casimir if he wished to join her entourage. "Perhaps you can find your roots there—the roots for your grapes?"

Casimir smiled enigmatically. "Why not?" And he shrugged his shoulders with infuriating indifference.

16

Eugénie hunted with spirit and loved to be in at the kill. She savored bullfights, which she would attend in scarlet boots, carrying a dagger or a whip instead of a fan. Her luscious red hair was casually sprinkled with gold dust, her furtive eyes accented with dark mascara, but her dusky expression and ethereal beauty rendered her an inaccessible desire.

She did not hesitate to take advantage of everything that *couture* could bestow upon her slim figure. For the journey to Suez, she ordered a new wardrobe of intricately brocaded crinolines from the couturier Mr. Worth, who had lately been threatened by the potential loss of her patronage since a fortune-teller had predicted that Eugénie would go to a distant land and fall in love.

Why not? After all, her husband, Napoléon III, was an incorrigible womanizer, possessing an immense sexual appetite. Why not even the score?

Dressed in his customary skullcap and furred robe, Mr. Worth personally pinned on Eugénie's slender waist the *tournure*, the drapery that gave women's hips a graceful curve. He called it the "crayfish tail," his new invention not yet revealed to the world of fashion.

He wanted her to promise she would return.

The Empress laughed. "*Je reviens*," she said. "I will return. Do I have a choice, Monsieur Worth?"

A constellation of rose, orange blossoms, vetiver, and cloves—that's what Worth extracted from Eugénie's words that afternoon. *Je Reviens*, a perfume concocted in the Worth distilleries with which every beautiful woman in Paris doused herself during her outings. And his competitor Creed countered with *Empress Eugénie*, a scent which still lingers, her immortality.

Monsieur Cazal made Eugénie more than a dozen new parasols of every color in paper and silk. Madame Gringoire at the Place Vendôme fitted her with the most voluptuously sculptured corsets. Chaumet crowned her with exquisite diadems. And Louis Vuitton, who was her personal packer, filled countless steamer trunks.

"I was born during an earthquake," she told him. "What would the ancients think of such an omen?

Surely they would have said I was fated to convulse the world. I believe in fate."

"So do the Turks," Vuitton told her, handing her a single gold key that opened every one of the trunks. "They call it *kismet*."

PART II

Journeying in search of romance,

and that, after all,

is our business in this world.

·~Joseph Conrad

17

On September 30, 1869, leaving her husband and only son at the Palace of Saint-Cloud, Empress Eugénie boarded the imperial train for Venice. She was accompanied by a flashy retinue, including the Duchess d'Albe, Mme. de la Nadaillac, Prince Murat, Général Douay, Comte Davilier, Comte de Brissac, Comte de Clary, Mlle. de Larminat, Mlle. Marion, Commandant Reffy, and Marquis de Châteauneuf.

Casimir was exhilarated to be facing East once again. Although he had long stopped dreaming of the woman with the blue and the yellow eye, she was permanently engraved in his consciousness.

The travelers arrived on the eve of October 2nd in Venice, where Surville, the captain of the imperial yacht, the *Aigle* (the Eagle—alluding to the Napoléonic crest), greeted them.

To celebrate their arrival, all the *palazzos* on the Grand Canal were illuminated from the inside, the Rialto adorned with brilliant red lamps, their lights shimmering across the waters. The peculiar undulation of the gondolas as though they were breathing in unison, their countless beaks reared up with strange curving crests like a field of dragons, created such an unseemly vertigo that the Empress felt light-headed.

The *Aigle* left Venice on October 7th, sailing out of the Malamocco Strait at midday. The sky was ominous with dark clouds, the wind was thrashing. But Casimir de Châteauneuf was not affected by the violence of the tumultuous sea.

On the 9th, the *Aigle* left the Adriatic. Following the coastline of the Ionian Islands, it reached Cape Matapan, where heavier sea and nasty North-Easterly winds prevailed.

Captain de Surville was anxious.

Queasy and apprehensive, the royal guests were confined to their cabins. The rough weather persisted in the Oro Canal, obliging the captain to slow down the engines as far as Tenedos so as not to tire the vessel and to avoid excessive water at the front.

"We must change course," he announced.

As the hope of ever reaching Constantinople began to

fade, the passengers gathered in the yacht's chapel in silent prayer. As if Poseidon had heard their inner voices, the winds soon departed. The clouds followed. The sea calmed.

At the same moment, a crescent moon and star came together in the sky as if the magic emblem of the Ottomans were celebrating their arrival.

The *Aigle* glided into the Dardanelles where the whole length of the strait, the banks, the batteries, and a fleet of vessels covered with multicolored lights, greeted them with booming cheers and gunfire. Steamships from every country, dressed with flags and stocked with people, moved in front of the Empress, to salute and escort her to her destination.

"At daybreak, we shall see the first minarets," Captain de Surville promised. "To arrive in Constantinople on a fine morning, believe me, *that's an unforgettable moment in one's life.*"

18

Through an arc of opaline mist, minarets burst, like fountains shooting skyward frozen into stone. The spectral outline of the gardens, the hills, the cypresses, and serried houses extended toward the Sublime Porte, the sacred site of the ancient acropolis.

On their right was Asia, on their left Europe. The view resembled the Grand Canal of Venice made colossal and situated on the Barbary Coast. Before them, a meandering expanse of water stretched, fringed with palaces and mosques, the seven hills glistening in the morning light like a strand of lapis lazuli.

Beyond the silhouette, the dark line of the ancient walls, uneven and tortuous, with seven massive towers at curious intervals, encircled the entire city.

They had arrived at the city of the world's desire.

19

The *froideur* of the Empress had unsettled the Sultan ever since making her acquaintance during his visit to Paris the year before. From the moment he met her, he had recognized in Eugénie's cool gaze the constraint of an unopened woman. A woman who had harvested all worldly goods but none of their heavenly pleasures.

He wanted her to know the colors, the joys his own wives knew. He wanted to show her a glimpse of desire.

He put at her disposal a palace of cut jasper along the Asian shores, amid magnolia-filled gardens. At Beylerbey, every piece of furniture was custom-made by the finest ebenists, every chandelier by the most gifted Murano. The walls of the royal suite were paneled with mother-of-pearl, tortoiseshell, and silver. As was the bed.

Beylerbey boasted the most opulent *hamam*, or

bathhouse, in Constantinople, covered with ancient Paros marble of earthly hues and centuries-old Iznik tiles. A vast stained-glass dome of ornamental grace hung over its scented pools.

The chief palace cook had been sent to Paris to hire chefs and waiters, acquire tableware, and study with the prodigy chef Escoffier. He took pride in inventing dishes that integrated the whims and wiles of both cuisines for the Empress. When Eugénie developed an instant appetite for eggplant, which she had never tasted before, he concocted "The Empress's Caprice." And the Sultan immediately ordered a coach, packed with a hundred varieties of eggplant seeds, to be sent to France.

He will lay the world like a red carpet in front of me so that I can walk, she thought. I see it in his eyes. "But where could we grow this *aubergine* vegetable?" she asked with uncustomary giddiness.

"In Provence, my lady," Casimir de Châteauneuf assured the Empress. "Not far from my own vineyards. Nightshades thrive better in that soil than anywhere else in the world. *Aubergine* will need a long dry sun."

Casimir remained awake on their first night, as if keeping vigil, sensing the intimation of an affinity he did not yet understand. He perceived a hidden freedom of language and behavior behind the subservience of this world of protocol.

He watched the ships that passed in the night. He

gazed across the bay at the illumination of the Dolmabahçe and the Çirağan palaces, the turrets of the Sublime Porte, rising in its confluence. He had an irrational desire to partake in the grand movement of this six-thousand-year-old city—Byzance, Constantinople, Istanbul.

"I have seen the crescent and the star over the Bosphorus. A cycle of my life closes," he had read somewhere.

It felt as though his own cycle of life were coming to a closure.

20

Despite her fatigue from traveling, Eugénie too stayed awake with childlike expectation.

At dawn the Sultan, who had remained in Beylerbey and awakened to the chant of the *müezzin*, encountered the Empress strolling alone in the scented garden. She seemed in perfect peace.

"The dew on the leaves," she told him in awe. "So like diamonds."

"It is their tears."

Eugénie caught his searching eyes, eyes that showed the depth of his sensuality, but also held a gleam of the fanatic. A haughty-looking man with lowered brows, Abdülaziz held a somber expression upon his dark visage. A touch of poetry and melancholy enshrouded him.

A day later, he returned on a white charger, scintillating with medals and a huge emerald aigrette on his fez. He gazed straight before him, deliberately oblivious of the cheering of the spectators, as the band played the "Sultan Aziz March."

It quickly switched to "La Marseillaise" while the Sultan dismounted his horse, walked toward Eugénie, and handed her an exquisite bouquet of white roses that he himself had grown. Concealed inside was an emerald leaf sprinkled with tear-shaped diamonds, the perfect imitation of a leaf with the dew.

"The tears!" she exclaimed. "I've never witnessed such beauty."

"Only eclipsed by your own. . . . Is there anything else you desire, My Lady?"

"Alas, only to visit the Grand Harem," she sighed. "Since I will never have the fortune of inhabiting one myself, I should very much like to visit."

21

In his court, Sultan Abdülaziz had five thousand five hundred courtiers (excluding their servants), one thousand horses, four hundred musicians, two hundred servants caring for his vast menagerie, four hundred workers in the kitchen, five hundred carriages, a Harem of fifteen hundred women, and that many eunuchs to guard them.

But not one woman in the Harem spoke a word of French. And none of the French ladies spoke the mystical Ottoman language. Naturally, no gentleman other than the Sultan would be allowed into the sanctum. If he were to fulfill Eugénie's wish, how were the women going to converse with one another?

The torchlights searched the city in the night. Then someone remembered. Wasn't there once a girl at the Palace of Tears, that melancholy place on the edge of

Topkapi palace, where the cast-away women of the pre-
vious Sultans lived in abandoned isolation? They called
her Kukla, which meant "doll" in their language, or La
Poupée, because once upon a time, she had been the
living doll of Aimée de Rivery, the legendary French
Sultana.

22

Aimée Dubucq de Rivery was the woman who had changed Kukla's life as Kukla had changed hers.

It was an old custom. Instead of dolls, princesses and courtly women were given little girls as gifts. Like human pets. The royal ladies made clothes for them, dressed and undressed them, gave them baths, and fed them. Through caring for their living dolls, they learned the domestic arts. And they learned to expose their hearts. Some taught their dolls skills of value. Some loved their dolls; others abused them.

Aimée de Rivery was steeped in loneliness and despair when a eunuch presented her with the little girl. What struck Aimée first were the peculiar eyes. One blue, the other yellow. Like an Angora cat. She took it to be an omen.

At first, she treated Kukla like a precious bird. She would feed her sweets and nuts and Kukla would open her mouth and swallow the morsels out of the Sultana's hands, pecking lightly and licking. Aimée received such pleasure in feasting her doll that her lips blossomed into smiles of a nature that no one had seen since her arrival at the palace. The gardeners heard her strange song drifting out of the tightly woven lattices:

Adieu madras, adieu foulard . . .

The child had been instructed not to speak a word to the Sultana. And, having already lived through formidable ordeals during the five short years of her existence, Kukla had come to grasp the wisdom of obedience. Good dolls kept silent and she had resolved to be a good doll.

Aimée de Rivery attributed this silence to the slowness of Kukla's wit, or lack of imagination in her soul, until the day she found her alone in the *hamam*, sitting at a marble sink and splashing water on herself.

Through the humid hollowness, the reverberations of the tiny voice echoed, amplifying into cloudlike forms of steam:

Adieu madras, adieu foulard
Adieu rob'soie, adieu collier choux

Doudou en moins li ka pâti
Hélas, hélas! Ce pou toujou

The child was singing a song that the girls sang to their sailor lovers in Martinique, with an uncanny Creole accent like Aimée's own.

Kukla knew words.

She knew how to imitate.

She had intelligence.

She had grace.

She was a cherub.

Non, non, non, non déjà top tard,
Bâtiment a déjà sur la bouée.
Non, non, non, non, déjà top tard,
bientôt il va appareiller.

Kukla continued singing. With laughter and tears, Aimée joined in her song. The two returned to the beginning for another round and many more to follow.

Adieu madras, adieu foulard.

23

Aimée de Rivery named the girl La Poupée and loved her like a favorite doll. Had it not been for the incentive to bring up the child in her own image, the sad Sultana might not have survived the coldness of the nightfall, the inky darkness, the loneliness of this heathen land.

She sewed her dresses fit for a princess. She put ribbons in her hair. She trained her in courtesy. Under the pretense of play, Aimée passed on to the child everything she herself had known in her tumultuous life. She taught her French, the language of her origins. To read and write and *Un, deux, trois*. She taught her other Creole songs. But more than all else, she told her stories in the secret language only the two of them shared in their gilded cage.

"On a faraway island named Martinique, on the Sea

of Caribbean, my family grew sugar. We were called Creoles," Aimée began.

She pulled out a map hidden under her mattress, the
one she had stolen long ago from the pirate ship, the one
she had sewn inside her skirt so that she could always remember where she was. She opened the map and showed
it to the child.

"You see right here in Trois Ilets. I had a cousin
named Joséphine (Maria-Josèphe-Rose Tascher de La
Pagerie) and we were very close. Perhaps, something to
do with the strong force ever present in the islands,
something dark, something supernatural that made us
seek refuge in each other.

"One day, while everyone was taking siesta, we crept
through endless rows of sugarcanes, under the white afternoon heat, looking for Euphémie David, the mulatto
fortune-teller. Euphémie lived in a tumbledown shack, its
path bordered down by lilies of all kinds, hibiscus, and
ginger but outshining all, clusters of *Amaryllis gigantea*.
See, just like the enormous red flowers growing outside
this pavilion that I myself planted."

"What did the fortune-teller say?" La Poupée asked.

"Oh, the poor woman gasped when she looked at our
palms. '*Mon Dieu*, what a supreme fortune each of you
have! I have never seen hands like this! *Mon Dieu*, you
shall both be Queens,' she exclaimed as she crossed her-

self. 'One to rule the East and the other the West,' and she knelt down before us and kissed our skirts.

"We giggled as this was what any young girl wishes—that she'll grow up to become a Queen—but naturally we didn't believe a word. Joséphine said, that must be what the woman tells all pubescent girls. We should not take it literally. But neither of us had a clue to what was to come, of course."

"What happened to Joséphine?"

"That spindly dark girl who once was like a sister . . . Joséphine married an officer named Beauharnais and moved to France. But when they guillotined him for treason . . ."

"What is guillotine?"

Aimée did not want to frighten the little girl with horrors of the external world. "Joséphine became the Queen of the West, the Empress of a distant country called France," she continued, and pointed at the map again. "She later married a tyrant named Napoléon Bonaparte, who lusts to swallow the world. Who has attempted to conquer Egypt. But alas, I never saw Joséphine again after I left the island."

"Why?"

"The day I sailed away from Fort-de-France toward Port Royal, my eyes caught a last vision of her among the brightly clad slaves, lined along the water, waving and singing *adieu madras, adieu foulard*—the first song you heard me sing, the one that bonded us. I waved back and, at that moment, I had a premonition that I was never to return.

"That same night, a glowing light appeared in the sky. A phosphorescent flame, Saint Elmo's fire, they called it. It attached itself to the ship and formed a halo around it like a wreath."

Aimée de Rivery then traced on the map the path of a ship crossing the Atlantic Ocean to the Brittany coast of France.

"Here is Nantes, where I attended the convent school, Dames de la Visitation. Eight years with the nuns. Then, finally, I had completed my studies and was to return to Martinique but never reached my destination."

"What happened?"

"Here, at the Bay of Biscay, a great storm broke. In the middle of the night the ship listed and began to sink. Suddenly, a galley of Algerian corsairs was alongside us."

The French Sultana moved her fingernail through Gibraltar, to the coast of North Africa, where the pirates had sold her to the Bey of Algiers. Then, along the coast of the Mediterranean again but in the opposite direction this time, passing the ruins of Carthage, the little white huddle of Sidi-Bou-Saïd, and the red earth of Tunis. Sicily, Greece, then, up to the Aegean, through a constellation of islands—the route of Ulysses through the Dardanelles, to the city of Constantinople, where the Bey had given her as a gift to the Sultan to win his favor.

"And so, I entered the Grand Harem. They changed my name to Nakshedil and here I sit in this gilded cage, the favorite of the Grand Turk, who rules the kingdom of the East."

And that was her story.

La Poupée listened intently. She did not remember her own past except for a vague trace of a small cottage and strangers who came in the night. "Where do I come from?" the child asked.

The French Sultana's fingers slid to the Eastern edge of Anatolia, beyond the Black Sea, and made a tiny circle around the Caucasus Mountains. "There, from the land of the ancient Amazons. You're a Circassian."

"But now I'm here. And you are too." Kukla pointed at the city of Constantinople on the map.

"Yes, we are both here, *ma Poupée*."

24

The women in the Harem were not allowed to read.

Aimée de Rivery manipulated the means to accumulate great volumes for her son, the Crown Prince, so that he would someday have a point of reference about the world. And, of course, so that she could pursue her own secret passion for books.

She hired scholars to copy manuscripts from other languages, as they did without comprehending the words, simply conforming to their calligraphy. And she hired translators to translate the Classics.

In the night, Aimée made La Poupée steal into the library to take a book. By candlelight, in excited whispers, she read to the child everything from the *Iliad* and the *Odyssey* (both of which had occurred in this land of exile) to *Medea* and *Salammbô*. During those hours, they followed in the footsteps of the great travelers, their own journeys confined to their interior lives, which seemed to expand deeper into the unexplored territories of their consciousness.

This is how La Poupée learned everything in the Sultana's old language. She learned to read, and this strange alchemy of symbols into images of the mind possessed her like religion. She learned to compose poetry, the art of rhetoric, and discourse. But since it was forbidden for women to acquire knowledge, especially in a heathen tongue, in the company of others she feigned ignorance. No one was to know the complexity of her mind. No one to suspect her other tongue, which relished stories as if they were the elixir of life.

"Even more than all the knowledge I've imparted to you and all the skills, the greatest wisdom will be to never let anyone know what you know. Silence will be your best accomplice, unless—"

"Unless?"

"Unless you enter the *rêve à deux*."

"What is *rêve à deux*?"

The Sultana did not tell her the meaning of *rêve à deux* then but instead read her three stories, although they had not been written. One was called "The Brushwood Boy," another "Peter Ibbetson," and the third "Usha's Dream."

"*Rêve à deux* is when you can have parallel dreams with another person."

"How?"

"You dream someone else's dream. And they dream yours."

The Sultana sighed, wandering off to her divan to enter her own *rêve à deux*, to reunite with the soul mate of her dreams. Of course, she kept this all to herself, not even confiding in La Poupée, who had already sensed that Aimée had another life elsewhere, peopled with beings that did not exist into this world. She also sensed that into this world of Aimée's, even she was not allowed to enter.

That night, lying in bed, La Poupée whispered to herself over and over again. *Rêve à deux. Rêve à deux*, until the repetitions whirled her into sleep.

25

It was around this time that a traveling French painter was making his way through Constantinople. His name was Nomad and he specialized in intricate miniatures.

Nomad had been employed by the Empress Joséphine to insinuate his way into the Sublime Porte and paint the portrait of the Grand Sultana. Joséphine had been curious and restless ever since receiving a diamond aigrette as a gift from the Sultana of the Ottoman Empire with the inscription *The Queen of the East embraces the Queen of the West.*

She had no doubt that a hidden message existed within the official gesture.

Only one person could allude to these words, the words that a fortune-teller in Martinique had once uttered: her cousin Aimée de Rivery. Her best friend in childhood. But the debris from poor Aimée's ship had washed ashore after a great storm. There were no survivors, only rumors that some had been kidnapped by a pirate ship.

Nomad spent enough gold to entice the necessary eunuchs to clear his path to paint the Sublime Porte. But, since no men were admitted into the Harem, he had the privilege of seeing the Sultana only through a tiny opening from the eunuchs' quarters. Ingeniously, he devised a camera obscura to paint her facsimile.

When Aimée saw her image, she was so enchanted by its delicate strokes, its lifelike quality that she asked the painter to make one of La Poupée, who was in the bloom of youth.

She dressed La Poupée in her own green caftan with golden tulips and wrapped a jeweled turban around her head. She instructed her to sit in perfect stillness, staring directly at a crack on the wall, for what seemed like eternity.

During these endless hours, La Poupée was disturbed by thoughts and sensations unfamiliar to her. Who was behind the wall? She imagined someone resembling the illustrations she'd seen of Tristan, Romeo, or Beau Geste. She imagined a gorgeous youth. What eyes do not see the mind creates more vividly.

She caught a glimmer of unknown joys, and was filled

with a terrible yearning. She could feel the painter's breath on the other side of the wall. He put his lips to the hole and whispered, "How beautiful you are!"

La Poupée had never heard the voice of a man before except the eunuchs' falsettos. The breath that rose, the sound of the male voice, the caressing tone of the French language unsettled her.

"But you must remove your garments, *ma belle*, so I can paint you the way God meant for you to be seen."

For a split second, La Poupée had the impulse to obey. To reveal her most private self to the world outside. But, quickly gathering her wits, she ran out of the room, and threw herself into an ice-cold pool.

For days after that, the thrill of the male did not diminish.

That's when the dreams began.

She dreamed of a prince from a distant land who climbed into her room, kissed her lips, and awakened her from the spell of an evil eye. *Je vous aime.* He spoke the language Aimée had taught her. Then, together, she and this prince traveled to a distant land on flying camels as if in a tale from *The Golden Voyage of Sindbad.*

She did not tell Aimée de Rivery of the dream but she did of the strange thrill.

Aimée felt a catch in her throat. She coughed and blood came.

She had not faced her mortality. She had never considered for La Poupée a future away from herself, because after all, *La Poupée* was her doll. No one else was entitled to her.

She had ignored the jealousies, the dark desires of the Harem, where all the women's vices and virtues played havoc. What would become of La Poupée if she were to expire? How would the women who had been jealous of her treat La Poupée?

It happened slowly. Day by day, Aimée faded a shade lighter until consumption erased her vibrant aura.

26

Father Christophe was kneeling in prayer at the convent of Saint-Antoine when two guards arrived in haste. They handed him a letter, stamped with the imperial seal.

The guards then escorted the priest down the steep and curvaceous streets of Pera to the landing in Galata where a splendid caïque awaited. It pushed away from the shore into an opaque fog, swiftly becoming a phantom.

On a marble scroll above the entrance to the Gates of Felicity, the inscription read:

> *May Allah preserve the glory of its possessor forever!*
> *May Allah beautify its buildings!*
> *May Allah strengthen its foundations!*

Father Christophe crossed himself. For the first time in history, a priest was entering the Sublime Porte.

He followed the guards through a courtyard, then a second gateway, through the Court of the Janissaries, the armory, the mint, the imperial stables, the birdhouse, the kitchens, the mosque.

Alighting before a small door carved with filigree, he was led by a eunuch through a long corridor, up a narrow stairway into the Harem.

On a sumptuous bed lay a pale woman. A young girl sat by her side, holding the woman's hand. "The Sultana wishes to die in her original faith. Please," she told the priest in French, and stepped into the shadows.

Father Christophe listened to the dying woman's confession until the words became whispers and at last faded away. He gave her absolution. As he uttered the words of Extreme Unction, a faint song escaped from the shadows:

Adieu madras, adieu foulard.

27

After Aimée's death, La Poupée sank into melancholy; she had lost words and found solace only in the pages of the books.

She possessed no skills the Harem could harness. She knew nothing of making sherbets, or dresses, nor did she have any training in erotica. Her only interest was tending the library.

She became its keeper.

Pulling the books off their shelves one by one, she would fondle each, tracing her fingers gently down its spine, caressing its binding, touching its skin with her lips. As the dustcloth rolled languidly on each page, her eyes wandered to the words that grew into sentences, that grew into paragraphs. And like this, she consumed each story.

Once, she counted the volumes. Exactly one thousand and one.

She set about memorizing each one.

But gossip snarled around the Harem like a tangled cat's cradle, the rumor that the late Sultana's doll could "read," that she had already read the books in the library and knew everything they contained.

The Chief Eunuch discovered La Poupée one night, candles lit all around her little alcove. She was reading to herself from Lady Montagu's journal and she continued out loud:

> Was I to follow entirely my own Inclinations it would be to travel, my first and chiefest wish. If I had a Compannion, it should be one that I very much lovd, and that very much lovd me, one that thought that it was not below a man of sense to take satisfaction in the conversation of a reasonable woman, one who did not think tendernesse a disgrace to his understanding.

The girl was obviously on the verge of madness and sacrilege.

28

La Poupée was condemned to the Palace of Tears for the rest of her life.

29

On that October night, some years later, as the searchers combed the city for a woman who could speak French, Empress Eugénie and her entourage dined privately at the French Embassy.

Across the Golden Horn, La Poupée lay on her mattress in the damp, dark cubicle she shared with five other young women, far from the palace of the French Sultana who had many years since gone to Paradise. She was now a young woman, well in her prime.

La Poupée lay awake, replaying the recurrent dream in her mind, the one in which she and her dream lover were riding flying camels in the sky. The dream that she had begun to dream when the *Amaryllis gigantea* had prematurely burst into scarlet bloom.

But even when she was awake, his face haunted her

every thought. From the instant their eyes first met, she recognized him as someone from another time, another world in which they had been intimate and inseparable.

La Poupée was still lying in bed, reconstructing the features of the man's face in her mind's mirror, when she heard a commotion outside. She opened her eyes, only to find herself an inmate in the mildewed dormitory with other castaway toys sleeping next to her.

The footsteps approached closer and closer. She was dragged out of bed, wrapped in a tunnel of silk, and guided through the mazes of the Palace of Tears, into a carriage.

As it rattled down cobbled streets, the night city glistened through the star holes of the lattices. She could even inhale the evening breeze over the Bosphorus.

Then, they stopped, wrapped another silk tunnel around La Poupée, and led her onto a barge. But where were they taking her?

She remembered the nights of abduction from the palace. She remembered the stories of hundreds of Harem women stuffed into sacks and thrown into the sea to fulfill the whim of an insane Sultan. She imagined an undersea forest of dead concubines.

But fear did not thrive in her heart. Just curiosity.

30

Two enormous iron gates opened into the courtyard of the new palace, which was called Beylerbey.

"But she's so frail," gasped the matron, struck by La Poupée's sallow skin, which had all the delicacy of a miniature painting. But also a greenish hue from the absence of the sun.

"Her eyes—one is blue, the other yellow," someone said. "Isn't that supposed to be bad luck?"

"But she's the only one who speaks the *Lingua Franca*!"

"Then, we must find a way to make her beautiful."

The women bathed and anointed La Poupée, fed her a large bowl of mutton stew and syrupy baklava. They hennaed her hair, her hands. They rubbed her skin with arnica so it would regain its glow.

In the morning, the greenness was gone although La

Poupée had not fully recovered herself. They put rouge on her cheeks and painted her lips bright red. They curled her hair in ringlets imitating Empress Eugénie's, piling them on top of her head like a bunch of grapes. They dressed her in an old caftan of Aimée de Rivery's, the green velvet one with the golden tulips, the one La Poupée had once posed in for the invisible artist who had spoken to her through a secret opening. The artist who had painted their portraits through a camera obscura. The artist who had excited her with his flirtatious words and made her aware of her heat. Who had then disappeared, and with him, the portraits. What had become of them?

When La Poupée caught her reflection on an enormous mirror, she saw Aimée de Rivery. Not her physical attributes but her charisma, the radiance of her spirit.

Except she had one blue eye and the other yellow.

3¹

How delightful!" one of the French ladies whispered to another. "Look how exotic her dress is!"

"Doesn't she remind you of Monsieur Ingres's odalisque?"

"But have you ever seen such eyes!"

The Empress asked the girl her name in French.

When La Poupée heard the secret language that the French Sultana had taught her, she blushed. "La Poupée, My Lady," she answered as she curtsied the way Aimée de Rivery had trained her.

"La Poupée?" The ladies repeated the Creole accent. They all laughed except the Empress, who was distracted by the young woman's peculiar eyes.

As was a figure in the balcony, behind the dark lattices.

Casimir de Châteauneuf stood transfixed like a statue. He was mesmerized by the young woman's voice. *Je vous aime. Je vous aime.*

"La Poupée," he repeated to himself.

There was no doubt. No doubt.

His body could not bear the impact of such proximity. His heart was about to explode from his body.

La Poupée was oblivious of Casimir's presence but she could sense that she had become an object of interest for the French ladies. She could feel her entire body language changing to accommodate the words released from her mouth. She sensed her old self returning to her, the self she had known with Aimée de Rivery. Even something more, as if inside her, two beings coexisted in perfect harmony.

What a mixture of a courtesan and a courtier, Eugénie mused to herself. "You seem well poised in courtly manners, Poupée."

La Poupée cast her eyes to the floor, keeping them fixed on the Anatolian carpet, woven with symbols of double goddesses and chevrons and rivers, losing herself in its intricate symmetry. She could still not understand why she had been brought here. She had passed the age of being "the doll" of another Empress. Who were these ladies, then, who spoke to her in Aimée de Rivery's language, and what did they want?

"Poupée," the Empress said to her. "It seems you are

the only woman who speaks French in this entire city. But tell us how you came to learn our language so well and with such a flavored accent?"

La Poupée unrolled the old map that was hidden in the seam of her underskirt and laid it on the floor. The crinolined ladies clustered around her.

"This is where Aimée de Rivery, the French Sultana, once lived—in the Trois Ilets. On a faraway island named Martinique, on the Sea of Caribbean. Her people were called Creoles," she began.

Everyone knew about Joséphine Bonaparte's cousin from Martinique kidnapped by Levantine pirates, never heard from again. Rumors floated that she had become the Queen of an exotic land. But everyone had taken this only for a legend. Such things did not occur in real life.

Everyone also knew of the diamond aigrette Joséphine had received from the Ottoman Sultana with the inscription *The Queen of the East embraces the Queen of the West*. They knew that Joséphine had tried to contact the Sultana but failed since the women in the Harem were denied the external world.

La Poupée held the French ladies under her spell. Her stories rolled like pearls out of her tongue as she conjured up a freedom of language the like of which she had never encountered. The words came faster, pouring from her center as if a floodgate had opened. The sounds found song in the air, sugar sweet like Martinique. Songs grew into ballads. *Adieu madras, adieu foulard.*

The voice she had distilled from reading all those volumes in the library had matured into one of a master storyteller.

The captive audience did not assume that La Poupée's stories were indeed about real people and places, neither did they care. They listened, wanting more. They had found their own Scheherazade.

So had Casimir de Châteauneuf, his heart fluttering, sensing the insinuation of a familiar yet alien world and restraining himself from acting too foolishly, too impulsively, now that he was undeniably face to face with his true destiny. He feared he would impoverish the power of his passions if he were to reveal them too soon.

Wait for your kismet to find you.

He fled outside for fresh air. He stripped his clothes and jumped into the Bosphorus, although he had been told that the undertow was dangerous. Lord Byron had once swum across the same strait. So could he.

32

As the ladies drifted down the Sweet Waters of Asia to attend a circumcision ceremony in one of the royal *yalis,* the Empress had asked La Poupée if there was anything she wished.

"Yes, My Lady. I should like to visit Aimée de Rivery."

The royal carriages transported them to a mausoleum near Santa Sophia, in the gardens of Mosque Mehmed the Conqueror.

The snow of pigeons encircled the dome. It was a glass *türbe* encased in lattice ironwork resembling an orangerie. Visible through the windows, now opaque with dust, the faded velvet blanket with gold embroidery of Aimée's sarcophagus. Outside, clumps of dead weeds concealed an inscription: *She, the beloved, who opened the Occidental gate . . .*

La Poupée knelt on the ground and cleared away the arid weeds. Then, out of her handkerchief, she pulled out bulbs of *Amaryllis gigantea,* which she proceeded to plant around the *türbe.* Tears rolled down her face.

The others watched in silence.

The Empress was enchanted with La Poupée, an amazing creature from a magical realm. The color of her eyes, the way she rolled her *r*'s as if she were tasting Turkish delight. The seriousness of her concentration.

What a sensation she would make in her court! A live toy. What better present to bring back to France from the Orient?

Eugénie imagined the effect such delicate intelligence could induce among her courtiers. How she could dazzle the guests at her *séries* at Compiègne with La Poupée's extraordinary stories and charming way of telling them. What scents Mr. Worth could distill from the essence of this exquisite being. *La Poupée.* What couture she could inspire. How Winterhalter could immortalize her on canvas.

And, alas, with dread, the last but not the least, how La Poupée might also fall victim to her husband's compulsive lickerousness.

33

Later that afternoon, the ladies boarded an imperial barge rowed by forty oarsmen in gold-embroidered jackets. As they approached Dolmabahçe, the Sultan's main residence, Eugénie wondered what Théophile Gautier had implied when describing it as "Louis XIV Orientalized..."

Long flights of marble steps led from the entrance to the water's edge and disappeared beneath the waves. The white palace, reflected in the shimmering water below, exuded a sense of power, pomp, and pleasure.

Led by a retinue of eunuchs, the ladies walked through a court of French parterres tended by European gardeners, then up the marble steps to the grand entrance, which suddenly bloomed into a crystal staircase. Two flights carpeted in imperial red joined in a common landing, then split again into a wraparound gallery. Hundreds of crystal balusters supported the banisters.

They passed through endless corridors, flooded with soft radiance, which in turn opened to enormous rooms, their walls covered with baroque frescoes and lit with domes of crimson crystal.

At last, they arrived at the largest throne room in Europe, where an alley of Corinthian columns supported a domed ceiling with *trompe l'oeil* clouds, garlands, and drapery.

The Sultan sat on the gilded throne, transported from Topkapi, which had served all his predecessors. He rose with that certain languor only monarchs are privileged to display, took the Empress's hand, and gestured to place a kiss.

The ladies stirred. (Rumors had been circulating that the Sultan and the Empress had fallen in love.) Eugénie blushed. They made a supreme couple.

On the other side of the Saint-Gobain mirrors, framed in Parisian bronze, was the Harem. Through a small latticed window, the Mother of the Veiled Heads watched her son do something he had never done before. Something to impress the Frenchwoman, obviously. Something he must have observed in their court. Something unforgivable. He gave his arm to the Empress.

Eugénie took it with a glint in her eyes that surpassed the courtesy of protocol.

The tall baroque cassia-wood doors opened wide and they crossed the threshold into the Harem.

The Mother Sultana, Pertevale, sat on a low divan surrounded by numerous ladies dressed in damask Harem pants, brocaded with silver flowers under smocks of silk gossamer with long sleeves, hanging halfway down the arms. On their heads, they wore caps embroidered with gold and silver, from which dangled large bouquets of jewels made to look like flowers. Their hair, divided into tresses and braided with pearls and ribbons, cascaded in full length behind.

When she saw her son arrive arm in arm with this skinny red-haired siren who looked as if she wore a big birdcage under her skirt, the Mother of the Veiled Heads sprang up with unexpected agility. She mimed the motion of spitting on the floor, then slapping the Empress's face.

Eugénie froze.

It was not a good beginning.

The Mother Sultana had the privilege of being righteous. After all, hadn't she invested her life in the protection of her son's well-being? Wasn't she the one who herself cooked the dozen hard-boiled eggs that he demanded for each meal? Who served them to him wrapped in a bundle of black silk stamped with her own seal? The one who had brocade carpets spread along the streets through which he walked on his way to the mosque?

Eugénie cast a pleading look at the Sultan. Abdülaziz muttered a few words to his mother in a strange language to which she answered with bulging eyes and an agitated voice.

La Poupée did not translate.

Eugénie stood stunned. What should she do? She was a guest. She could not simply turn her back and walk out. What if she were to return the insult?

The Sultan motioned the French ladies to the divan to his right and the Harem ladies to the divan to his left. Then, he saluted and left them to themselves.

"There's a difference between your ways and ours," La Poupée whispered to the Empress in French. "One must never cross the Mother of the Veiled Heads."

"But I cannot let this moment go down in history."

"It already has, My Lady. We must now sit down and take tea with the Mother of the Veiled Heads."

The women sat quietly for an interminable minute, separated in their curiosity, as odalisques served tea and sweets.

They inspected each other's jewelry and clothes and hair.

Sounds of stirring tea. Crunch of biscuits.

The French ladies smiled in order to put the Turkish ladies at ease but received little response.

Nous sommes presque une famille, Eugénie uttered into the glass silence with a new attempt at dignity.

"We are almost a family," La Poupée translated in perfect imitation of Eugénie's voice.

"You see, my husband's uncle, Napoléon Bonaparte, was married to Joséphine, who was the cousin of Aimée de Rivery."

La Poupée translated again.

"There was no such person," the Mother of the Veiled Heads declared with righteous indignation. "The Franks contrived the whole story about Nakshedil Sultana being Aimée de Rivery because they want to own us."

"There was no such person as Aimée de Rivery," La Poupée translated back.

"Whose grave did we visit this afternoon, then? Your ability to speak French so well and with such an accent, doesn't it prove she existed?" Eugénie slurred her words. She was impatient.

"Yes, My Lady. But each of us experiences life differently. And we each have many secret lives, and some of our worlds are invisible to others."

The Crown of the Veiled Heads became irritated by the persistence of a tongue she could not understand. Incapable of making the distinction between the translation and the translator, she transferred the contempt she felt toward the Empress to La Poupée.

The girl had to be a *giaour*, the heathen Empress's spy. She should not be allowed in their company to get further corrupt ideas. She should be sent back to the Palace of Tears.

"What did she say?" she asked La Poupée.

"The Empress said, she herself doubted the story as well."

"Then, why make such a discourteous comment?"

"Because the Empress thought she was being polite."

Just then, hundreds of clocks began all at once to chime five rounds. The commotion of the mechanical monkeys, cuckoos, musical melodies agitated the air. Abruptly, the Mother Sultana sprang up again, along with her ladies-in-waiting, and they shuffled out of the room as if they had a more important mission.

"What must we do now?" Eugénie asked La Poupée.

"We must finish drinking our tea."

So the French ladies sat there by themselves and in silence sipped their tea.

34

The feast in the ceremonial hall for five hundred guests promised the most adventurous mélange of the East and the West. The twenty-two courses contained an entire range of animal impulses. Even the names evoked passion:

Potage Sévigné
Paupiette à la Reine
Croustade de foie gras à la Lucullus
Croustade d'ananas en Sultane
Suprème de faisan à la Circasienne
Bar à la Valide
Lips of the Beauty
Odalisque's dimple
La Voix de Roxalena

Lady's navel
The thigh of a Kadin
ƹ ƪ

Casimir stood with the rest of the gentlemen sipping champagne as the band played passages from Mozart's *Abduction from the Seraglio*. Casimir recalled the libretto, of Belmonte coming to rescue his beloved Konstanze from the evil Pasha who had abducted her.

Suddenly everything hushed for an instant as the Empress was announced and the band began playing Beethoven's *Turkish March*.

Eugénie walked in, dressed in a silver gown with low décolletage. Her diadem was of perfect diamonds and pearls and on her breast sparkled the greatest diamond of all, the Regent, which belonged to the Crown of France.

La Poupée followed, taking small, awkward steps behind Eugénie. She was wearing a royal blue crinoline dress, a gift from the Empress for the occasion (Mr. Worth's label, of course). But, since men were present in the room, she was veiled.

She moved as if she were gliding. The hall dazzled her, full of princes, ambassadors, elegant foreign ladies. She had never been in the company of men before.

Casimir could not steer his gaze away from La Poupée. The colors of her eyes were even more striking in reality.

At dinner, the Sultan, seated next to the Empress, reminisced about his visit to Paris with his two nephews—the first time any Sultan had traveled to a European city. He was so charming, in an honest, earthy sort of way, and even though he did not possess a clue to the cultivated game of flirtation, he had a certain Eastern Mediterranean virility that her own courtiers lacked.

He also had a Harem of many wives and concubines. Not that different from her husband, Napoléon III, really, who boasted only one wife but many mistresses.

Eugénie recalled Mr. Worth's prediction that she would fall in love in the Orient. *Je reviens*. She had never achieved a level of trust for a man that would allow her to make such a choice. An Empress should never lose her composure.

The afternoon tea in the Harem had restrained her imagination. She found herself facing a greater challenge, each time a new course was offered.

"I'm afraid the Mother Sultana could have poisoned my food," she whispered so a few of her intimates could hear.

"I will gladly taste your food, My Lady," La Poupée volunteered, accustomed to performing that task for Aimée de Rivery time and again with no qualm.

"No, *I* beg the honor of being your food taster, My Lady," someone else interrupted. "Allow me, My Lady."

The voice! La Poupée felt a warmth that washed all

over her. She raised her head and her eyes met Casimir de Châteauneuf's. There was no doubt. None.

Cupid's dart flew across the space. They recognized each other. It was love they were seeing, the consolation of the human race, the preserver of the universe, the soul of sensitive beings—tender love.

"La Poupée," he whispered.

The world disappeared. She could not distinguish between life and the dream. She slowly lowered her eyes but the mosaic of abstractions on the wall made her dizzy. She lost her balance and collapsed on the tiled floor.

Casimir de Châteauneuf instinctively reached to lift her up. Eugénie shook her head. *She should not be touched. In this world, a man's touch could be the kiss of death.*

Casimir retreated, allowing the Chief Eunuch the honors.

35

That night, as La Poupée lay in her airy room at the Beylerbey, the dream visited her again. She stole through the corridors and down the stairways of the slumbering palace, bypassing the drowsy eunuchs, and headed for the nightingale pavilion.

It was a night of honey. A full moon in the sky. One could kiss the moisture in the air. Everywhere, white opium blossoms blew flaccid in the soft breeze. The yellow laburnum drooped in full bloom and jasmine bushes spiraling around the gazebo stirred with insect lust.

Casimir de Châteauneuf awoke at the same moment, chasing the same dream. He raced through the grove of lindens to the pavilion.

In the gazebo he saw the silhouette standing alone.

His heart was pounding with the anticipation of the inevitable as he mounted the steps.

"La Poupée!" he called out.

"Je vous aime."

"Je vous aime."

Their hands found each other, and their lips. Their bodies, extensions of each other, moving as one. No lies. No boundaries.

36

Eugénie was agitated that night, jolted by the intensity of emotions displayed in this Eastern world. Everything seemed to possess such erotic nuance, such hints of violence.

She opened the doors to her terrace for fresh air. The opposite shore sparkled with the Sultan's palaces: Dolmabahçe, Çirağan, Beylerbey, Palace of the Stars, the Sublime Porte, the Topkapi . . .

She heard light footsteps. The moon was so bright that she had to shield her eyes. A veiled figure of a woman, she conjectured from the delicacy of the movement, scurried down the avenue of magnolias like an apparition.

A man followed the path in the opposite direction.

The Empress knew. She had perceived the mysterious magnetism between the two at the banquet.

She walked down to the fountain room, which connected the men's quarters to the women's, as Casimir arrived.

"Are you searching for your roots in the Sultan's garden, Casimir de Châteauneuf?"

"Just the fruits, My Lady."

"Exceptional, isn't she? I should like to take her back to Paris with me." The Sultan had been responsive to her in every way. He was courting her. Why should he deny her a present of La Poupée? "She should not be wasted here where they could not recognize her worth."

"You cannot transplant such a flower. She would wilt and perish in our courts. She lacks any sense of intrigue. She would be cannibalized," Casimir spoke firmly.

Eugénie recognized in his eyes that certain look of transcendence. "You must ignore the dictates of your heart, Casimir de Châteauneuf. It is too disastrous. You must know, as well as I do, that to covet a personal possession of the Sultan would not be a compliment but an insult."

"Then, it seems neither of us is entitled."

"That is the business of diplomacy."

"It is the business of fate, My Lady."

37

The next morning La Poupée was gone.

One of the attendants told Eugénie that, just before sunrise, she had woken up with what sounded like a night bird's cry. She had seen silhouettes of men leading a veiled woman to a caïque. The woman had resisted but had been silenced and taken away.

"The Mother of the Veiled Heads," Eugénie said. "She is punishing me."

Casimir de Châteauneuf paced up and down the corridors with intense concentration. La Poupée was gone. Just as he had found her. She was gone.

"It looks like fate has betrayed us both, Casimir. What will you do now?"

"I will do anything in order for it to reclaim me."

38

At his hunting lodge near the Black Sea, the Sultan invited the French gentlemen to shoot wild cocks. His passion for exotic birds was not a secret.

Being a sharpshooter and trained in the ways of the hunt, Casimir de Châteauneuf played his skill to the hilt. He needed to win the Majesty's confidence. The Majesty was duly impressed.

Casimir was aware that it was forbidden in the Orient for men to talk of women, even when surrounded by mist and gunsmoke. Yet speaking in enigmatic circles, a common game in both their traditions, allowed such trespasses.

"What happens to 'living dolls' when they come of age?" he asked the Sultan.

"They still remain the property of their mistresses."

"And should any misfortune befall the mistress?"

"Then, a marriage would be arranged."

"Always?"

"Almost always. Unless a rule has been betrayed."

So that was it.

"A rule such as?"

"Such as, having learned things that belong to the realm of men."

"Then what?"

"The Palace of Tears."

"What is the Palace of Tears?"

"The Palace of the Unwanted Ones."

"What is the exit from the Palace of Tears?"

"A great sacrifice."

"And then?"

"Don't ask me any more questions like that, de Châteauneuf. You are a heathen. You are not allowed to enter our *jennet*."

"Does not every man live many lives?"

"Of course, but he has only one kismet."

39

Casimir de Châteauneuf told the Empress that La Poupée was in the Palace of Tears and of his intention to remain in Constantinople.

Eugénie neither smiled nor offered a solution to calm his heart.

"We all fall in love," she said. "And we all suffer from the fall as love's sacrifice eventually catches up with us. Then, what is left? The challenge, my dear Casimir, is to flee from it while the embers are still glowing."

40

Before they sailed for Suez, Casimir de Châteauneuf gave Eugénie a personal letter to be delivered to Ferdinand de Lesseps, who was already in Egypt awaiting her arrival. Inside the envelope were two others: one addressed to a man in Paris at Quai aux Fleurs, who dealt in exotic birds. The other to his mistress, the one with the red mane and small, voluptuous lips who lived above the arcades in the Palais Royal.

"What makes you so certain that the letters will reach their intended recipients?" Eugénie asked Casimir. She resembled a smoking sphinx.

"It has never been certainty that motivates the will, My Lady."

41

The *Aigle* left for Alexandria on the 19th of October at ten in the morning.

The Sultan showered Eugénie with lavish parting gifts, among them a gilded sword for her husband, Emperor Napoléon III, with the inscription *Il y a deux choses importantes pour un empereur: pèse et vainc.* (There are two important things for an emperor: weigh the balance and win.) But those around him, who understood the double entendre, wondered if it was a calculated insult.

In Turkish, *pezevenk*, which sounded like *pèse et vainc*, meant a "pimp."

Casimir stood on the quay, watching the yacht glide toward the Aegean. He felt an estrangement, as if with it disappeared the man he had been.

From his bedroom window in Dolmabahçe, the

Sultan also watched. He was struck with profound melancholy for everything he had ever lost. He had considered detaining Eugénie. He could not reconcile this sublimation since tradition prohibited the taking of another's woman. Except, of course, as a condition of war which, in moments of delusion, Abdülaziz imagined in Napoléonic proportions.

Eugénie did not take La Poupée with her. She had not dared approach the Sultan with the request. Through some fragile insight, she had understood that it would be bad faith to cross the Mother of the Veiled Heads.

Instead, she took with her drawings of the windows at Beylerbey, to duplicate for her bedroom in the Tuileries. She wished always to remember how it had felt to gaze at the magnificent view across the Bosphorus and to recall that interstice of sensuality. And to remember the monarch poetic enough to make diamonds out of the dew.

42

Thomas Cook's *Excursionist and Tourist Advertiser*, July 1, 1869:

> On November 17th, the greatest engineering feat of the present century is to have its success celebrated by a magnificent inauguration fête, at which nearly every European royal family will have its special representative. Truly the occasion will be an exceptional one.... Everything connected with [the modern] works are on the most gigantic scale, and a perusal of a little pamphlet, descriptive of the undertaking, from the pen of the Chevalier de St. Stoess, impresses us most forcibly with the genius of the great Master-mind—Monsieur Ferdinand de Lesseps—to whose perseverance, calm daring and foresight, the dream of ages has at last become a real and tangible fact ... the project for bringing more closely together the East and the West, and thus uniting the civilizations of different epochs.

43

Khedive Ismail, the Viceroy of Egypt, was a formidable host. To celebrate the merging of the waters he had arranged visits to the pyramids, journeys up the Nile, exotic operas. *Aïda* was scheduled to have its premiere but since Verdi was not able to complete it on time—much to his chagrin—the guests had to settle for *Rigoletto*.

Thousands attended the lavish inaugural ball. Never so many crowned heads were seen together in one place.

Empress Eugénie, in her customary manner, made a dramatic entrance in a stunning red gown embroidered with diamonds—Mr. Worth's, naturally—the skirt slightly raised and gathered in the back. Underneath, a corset shaped like an hourglass set its own contours. Such also then was the inauguration of the *tournure,* about to become the latest rage with the ladies everywhere. Even in the Harem.

Among the tourist elite was a retinue of distinguished artists who came to record "the great pilgrimage of civilization" and went on the cruise down the Nile on the *Beheira*.

"Invited in the evening to tea with the Empress. This amiable woman has no heart; she's charming and hard, not to say cruel," remarked Fromentin, the great painter of the desert.

On November 17, 1869, the canal opened for navigation between Suez and Port Said. The waters gushed toward each other like lovers who had been separated forever. The lovely hand of Eugénie cut the symbolic ribbon, the umbilicus, thus raising the union of the two seas into the sphere of the eternal feminine.

The *Aigle* led the procession which streamed down the virgin canal, followed by an impressive cortège of merchant- and warships. In the evening, they dropped anchor at Ismailia on Lake Timsah, where the Viceroy had prepared more exotic festivities.

The next day, they reached the Bitter Lakes. The flotilla drifted out of Suez into the Red Sea.

"We fought, disposed, created, achieved, recognized, acted, persevered, advanced, succeeded," reverberated Ferdinand de Lesseps's strong baritone. "Nothing was impossible. Nothing could stop us. Ultimately nothing else mattered but the final result, *le grand but*."

Eugénie leaned back against the *Aigle*'s guardrail, holding a parasol in her gloved hand, and thought that the work could never have come to fruition without her influence behind the scenes. She deserved the credit for Lesseps's success. As had been prophesied, she was indeed convulsing the world.

The "piercing of the Isthmus" thus eliminated not only the four-thousand-mile trip around Africa, but a great nautical tradition that had been part of humanity for nearly five thousand years.

PART III

To want a world is fire—

to obtain it, smoke.

·~Gypsy proverb

44

Casimir de Châteauneuf traveled south to Smyrna, where, not long ago, he had almost perished. How close to his dream he had been! He had come to accept that something existed stronger than his will.

From Smyrna, he ventured to the interior of the Aegean, where thousands of haphazard vineyards sprawled up terraced hills, where Dionysus and his consorts had once gamboled. These were the same stock of grapes that the Etruscans had transported to the West.

With the local growers, he negotiated for the highest-quality rootstock, hearty enough for grafting and resilient to *Phylloxera*.

From the port of Smyrna, he shipped cratefuls of these strangely contorted roots, destined first for Marseilles, then for Grange du Souvenir in Châteauneuf-du-

Pape—with explicit instructions to the estate manager on the best grafting technique.

He also sent three young camels, one each for Antoine, André, and Alphonse. (The camels one occasionally encounters in the south of France are descendants of the same.) And for Espérance, a sachet of floral seeds. *Adonis* for sorrowful memories, *raspberry* for remorse, and *blue scilla* for forgiveness and forgetting, all in the wistful knowledge that she did not know the language of flowers but they knew hers.

45

At the Palace of Tears, La Poupée's mind remained incessantly preoccupied with the man in the garden. Had she actually seen him or had it been a dream within a dream? The intensity of the fleeting moments they had shared had become her sustenance, stretching beyond the dreamtime.

She asked the other women, "Have I been gone?"

They said her bed had been empty for some nights. But where she had been, they could not guess.

La Poupée told them then of her secret, although it was a risk to reveal such things. She told them of the French Empress and the elegant ladies in beautiful clothes and the funny hoops they wore underneath their skirts, called *crinolines*. And the gentlemen in knee breeches. She told them of the royal blue dress that the Empress had allowed her to wear. She told them of the Sultan's banquet, of the marble palace he had disposed for the Empress, and the emerald leaf with the diamond tears. She told them about planting the amaryllis bulbs at Aimée de Rivery's tomb. Of the Mother Sultana "slapping" the Empress, and of her own collapse.

Last she spoke about the man, the man whose name she still did not know but to whom she returned every night in her dreams.

She wept for the life she could never have. The other women cried too and asked La Poupée to tell them of the kiss again and the touch of the man, never having experienced such things and knowing they were not meant to. Not in this lifetime. *Kismet* is *kismet*. Written on one's forehead.

With each word, the face of her beloved appeared in La Poupée's mind's eye, as they had embraced in the nightingale pavilion. All other thoughts vacated her to focus on this single moment. All other words froze in her head except for *je vous aime, je vous aime*, the only words they had exchanged. She sang them over and over until the repetition bestowed a feeling of peace and she fell asleep to retrieve the same dream.

Gradually, La Poupée resigned herself to the Palace of Tears and a life without light. Now, all the women in the hollow chambers of the palace were heard humming, *je vous aime, je vous aime*. And all the eunuchs from their quarters whispering in their falsetto voices, *je vous aime, je vous aime*.

46

Casimir de Châteauneuf returned from Smyrna to Constantinople. He rented a small *yali* in Tarabya, overlooking the Bosphorus.

Every day, he sat cross-legged on the floor across from a Sufi master assigned to teach him the Koran at the Mosque of the Stars. Determined to decipher its complex calligraphy, he repeated incantations in words he did not yet understand but grasped with a visceral intelligence. Never for a moment did this seem absurd. Paradox had always overpowered meaning in his life.

The Sufi exorcised him of all past afflictions, the Catholic conventions and ceremony. He lit incense, chanted benedictions that freed Casimir of his past, even his name. In no time, the Frenchman spoke the language of the Ottomans with an impeccable accent and could read the Koran. *Amor vincit omnia.*

He cast away his dandy clothes in favor of a Stambouline, a black frock, and a fez with a red tassel. He grew a mustache like a Turkish gentleman. He frequented cafés where he played backgammon with the locals and smoked a water pipe. He learned to sing in the minor key.

Like a skilled actor, he came to reinvent his identity.

He now thought of himself as Cassim Bey, the name assigned him by the Sufi master for completing his teachings. The man who had been Casimir de Châteauneuf retreated into a fictional world.

Cassim Bey sat down to write a letter to Espérance. And to Antoine, André, and Alphonse. How to explain Casimir's desertion? No words came. Already, he was beginning to forget their faces, only their voices lingering in the hollow echoes of his memory.

*

☾

47

The birds arrived.

The dealer in Paris sent Cassim Bey a pair of each: the Chinese and the Malays, Cochin Chinas and Shanghais, the Gypsies and the Javas, Heghorns and Lamonas, Crevocouers and Creepers, Topknots and Gold Pheasants, White Leghorns and Rhode Island Reds, the Polish and the Hamburgs, Black Spanish and Bantams, Minorcas and Andalusians, Sumatras, and, of course, Sultans.

With the cages in tow, Cassim Bey made his way to the Palace of the Stars. The Sultan's penchant for collecting exotic chickens was common knowledge. Besides, the rumor hinted that "the convert" rewarded the men who cleared his path.

When Cassim Bey entered the darkly curtained Crown room, Abdülaziz was sitting on a Louis XIV chair. He appeared moody and taciturn, struck to stone with *mal de siècle*, wavering between weariness of the soul and a wretched state of apprehension. Later, Cassim Bey would recall that it was as though the Sultan were seized with an agitated foreboding of the tragic fate which awaited him.

Like a large amphibian that seems asleep but is not, he stared at Casimir de Châteauneuf, the intense French gentleman he had once hunted with, the same man who had so badly wanted that Poupée girl at the Palace of Tears. Love's foolishness. What else would compel the heathen now to masquerade in a Stambouline like his own courtiers? Nevertheless, the man before him was still a souvenir of the evanescent Eugénie, the unattainable object of his own desire.

"I have accomplished the great sacrifice, Your Highness. I'm now known as Cassim Bey," Casimir told the Sultan in Turkish.

"And in such a short time! But a few words of our language and our costume do not necessarily grant you the permission to be one of us, Châteauneuf."

"I *have* become one of you, my whole self. I *will* become even more so in time, Sire. It's my kismet."

"If you remain here, you can never return to your country, Châteauneuf. A man could be condemned to death by holy law if he were to revert to Christianity. By becoming a Moslem, you'd be losing not only your former faith, but also your name, your family, and your country. You are no longer the same."

"I am aware of that."

"One should never make a decision one may later regret."

"But then we would be trapped in a world without hope."

"Tell me, then, the real purpose of your visit."

Cassim Bey reached into his vest pocket and pulled out a green velvet box embroidered with tulips. "A few years ago, I found this in a curiosity shop in Paris."

The Sultan opened the delicate box and looked at the miniature of the young woman with vellum-toned features. One eye was blue, the other yellow.

He envied the Frenchman's determination and the freedom which allowed him that. He contemplated the portrait for a long time, then put the miniature in its box and handed it back to Cassim Bey.

"I'm a man of honor. I will grant you your wish. And, as homage to your estimable Empress, I'll grant you as dowry a ward in Macedonia. However, I warn you, there is nothing on the land but a hunter's shack. Ten acres of vineyards were planted there some years ago but yielded not one drop of wine. I've been told you're a master winemaker. Show me what you can do, Cassim Bey, with your ingenuity and imagination. Change the grapes to gold. Only then perhaps might I be able to take you seriously."

The Sultan stood up unexpectedly and opened the French doors to the adjacent reception hall. An audience of chickens and roosters, squawking and fluttering, congregated around the sovereign's feet. His face lit up like a child's. He could play soldier with them. He could give them honors. Catching hold of an enormous red rooster, he hung the medal of gallantry around its neck.

Cassim Bey watched.

"They tore down a Sufi temple to build this palace and now their imams tell me it will bring me bad luck," the Sultan told the frightened bird. "I believe in such omens. Don't you? Should we then consider moving to another palace, Your Highness?"

The rumors of the Sultan's mental demise had not been unjustified. But Cassim Bey had won his bounty.

48

That night La Poupée had another dream. The Mother of the Veiled Heads had sent "them" to take her away. She was dressed in bridal red. A carriage awaited her outside the Palace of Tears. It rattled along the city walls toward the Seven Towers.

It was still dark when she awoke. The *müezzin* was chanting the dawn prayer. A sense of *déjà vu* swept over her. She had lived this day before. She knew that the Seven Towers was the imperial prison from which there was no escape. But she experienced an unusual sense of peace.

Like a sacrificial lamb, she sauntered to the *hamam* for a ritual bath, then anointed her body with her own concoctions of herbal salves and floral scents. Ceremoniously, she slipped on the red dress that Aimée de Rivery had given her, then the ruby necklace and earrings with fire opals that had also once adorned her mistress.

Just as the dream had warned, a eunuch announced that "they" had come to fetch her. She kissed her friends, bade them farewell, and gave them everything she owned.

A trail of tears followed her through cold corridors of the Palace of Tears, but once again she felt the rush of running through a silk tunnel as if gliding in a translucent cocoon.

At the Gate of Felicity, a carriage awaited her. The eunuch helped her climb inside, then shut the door.

49

The carriage rattled down the cobbled streets toward the massive city walls. First, it went down the Grand rue du Seraglio, then crossed the square of Saint-Sophia, the Blue Mosque, the Baths of Arcadius, and stopped short before the Hippodrome.

"Continue!" a man's voice cried from within.

As soon as it reached the Burnt Column of Constantine and the Light of Osman Dome, it set off downhill and entered the Valley of the Mosques at a gallop.

At the sprawling aqueduct of the Emperor Valens, composed of two tiers of delicate arches around which vines trailed in graceful festoons down to a clutter of houses, the coachman wiped his brow, put his hat between his knees, and slowed down.

The carriage trundled now by the water's edge, along the towpath paved with sharp stones, heading in the direction of the Slave Bazaar beyond the Slaughter Square, where the massacre of Janissaries had occurred.

Then, it circled beyond the seventh cohort of Hebdomon and turned unexpectedly onto the bridge that traversed the little river Lycus toward Eyüp. In front of the garden of Ortacilar, the carriage came to a halt.

"Continue on!" ordered the voice again.

The coachman whistled his horses into a trot down an avenue of plane trees which led to the Ghetto of Constantinople, a quarter filled with decay and ruin and melancholy. By the time it reached Blacharnea, where the turreted walls of the Seven Towers extended from the Golden Horn across to the Marmara Sea, the driver was almost weeping with thirst and fatigue.

People on the street cast curious looks at the carriage with curtains drawn over its lattices, shut tighter than a coffin. At some point, a delicate hand drew the curtain and cast out some white petals, which scattered in the wind, flying away like butterflies over a vast field of red poppies.

And the driver heard a man's voice.

Je vous aime.

Je vous aime, a woman's voice replied.

As the sun sank over the Adrianople Gate, the carriage

stopped. A man got out and gave his arm to a veiled
woman dressed in bridal red.

Gazing at him with adoring eyes, she asked him,
"What is your name?"

50

Through Rumelia, Cassim Bey and La Poupée joined a camel caravan. Cassim Bey was determined to indulge La Poupée's recurrent dream of flying camels as it had already become an important part of their shared mythology.

They labored across the sunflowered expanse of Thrace, by way of Çatalca and Dimotika to the wastelands of Greece, and continued on to Drama and Saray, crossing the river Vardar and eventually cutting through the vampiric netherlands of Macedonia. They rested overnight in dubious inns and caravansaries, where Casimir kept watch with his hand on his dagger, while La Poupée feigned sleep.

The delicious torment of restraint in such proximity

only heightened their passion for each other. Their bodies were aflame and they impatiently anticipated the moment when at last they would be alone to touch.

Two weeks later, they crossed the Crna River and arrived in Pirlepé.

51

The wind was mean, the soil pale and full of stones. The air a whirling cloud of dust. The sad and sagging vines showed no promise of crop. All was sepia. No color.

Cassim Bey shot a wild boar that came charging and it became their sustenance for the winter. He labored to keep them warm, chopping wood, insulating the cabin with birch bark. La Poupée gathered plants and consistently cast a spell over their simple world with her stories.

The lovers were so filled with each other and the consummation they had not expected in this lifetime that the tribulations of a rough winter escaped them.

In each other's arms, they spent endless hours. Never had two natures conjoined and fused so intensely. Every moment had become like the night they had first dreamed of each other, drifting through cycles of desire, in and out of forbidden realms as if lured by the rhythm of a primeval dance.

Any moment apart was torture, even in sleep. Slowly, they learned to enter each other's dreams. Lying deliciously entangled in the desolate countryside encased in whirling clouds of dust, they shared dreams within dreams, chasing each other through a hall of mirrors that seemed to stretch into infinity.

They had entered the *rêve à deux*.

52

La Poupée's affinity for harvesting the earth's gifts did not tolerate killing the mountain goats and the wild doves for food. She craved the juicy tomatoes, bitter eggplants, and olive trees of her past.

Every morning, she traveled to the Silent Lake and brought back algae and shells, which she stirred into the stubborn soil. She buried seeds here and there. Pail by pail, she replenished the dried well from the Horse's Spring. All day long, she carried on incessant conversations with the *peris*, the plant spirits, visible only to her.

In the spring, the rains came, bringing unexpected fecundity. The seeds cracked and burst into double leaves, then multiplied. Flowers opened, leaves budded. Shrubs, saplings, and fruits thrived.

Cassim Bey watched La Poupée converse with the

plants, charming them as if snakes. He saw her make the ferns uncurl. He saw her swirling wildly in the woods as if possessed by an invisible force. All this excited but frightened him.

At the end of the season, the valley was verdant. With all this bounty, they could have lived in bliss forever. But Cassim Bey had never been a man of simple tastes. He stared at the limp, undernourished vines.

He imagined how La Poupée's horticultural gifts could themselves be harvested.

"We're going to make wine," he told her.

"What is wine?" she asked.

"The blood of the gods." He pointed at the struggling vines. "If we could only find a way to revive these!"

53

La Poupée spent interminable hours in the vineyards, communing with each vine as though it were her child. Not since dusting the books in the library and losing herself in their pages had she known such bliss. Cassim Bey looked on, mystified, uncertain whether she was a woman of magic or madness.

He told her about the soil, the angle of the sun, the hazards of frost and rain. He told her of squeezing the grapes and the art of fermentation. He watched her in amazement as she walked the aisles chanting, *"Grenache, Syrah, Cinsault, Counoise, Clairette, Muscardin, Mourvedre, Picpoule, Vaccarese, Rousanne, Bourboulenc."*

It made Cassim Bey smile. The words of grapes that she had no association with but owned as hers because they were his. He joined her chant, his lips synchronizing with hers, their duet reverberating to the valley below.

Day and night, he worked with the local coopers to build oak barrels. He monitored the progress of the crops, tested for acidity, sugar levels, pH balance, and phenol. The climate responded in perfect harmony.

Acres of vines spread down the knoll all the way to the Silent Lake. The gnarled branches rose as if in an erotic dance, swirling their arms in circles and arabesques.

At last, they burst forth with leaves, each of the brightest green. In the autumn, when an orgy of reds and burnt quince ravished them, Cassim Bey and La Poupée chanted in ecstasy as they ran along the rows of succulent grapes and fell down to earth, rolling on top of each other, in a frenzy of laughter, lost in the skin, their hands and lips seeking an even deeper fertility.

54

Cassim Bey sat on the veranda drinking his first harvest of *Orientalia* with its velvety texture and lively charm, its racy acidity and spicy bouquet. He recalled the smells and tastes of Châteauneuf-du-Pape. Grange du Souvenir. And Espérance. André, Antoine, and Alphonse. He heard their voices. For a brief moment even their faces appeared to him.

He wondered if they had received the gifts from Smyrna, the flower seeds, the camels, and the rootstock. He wondered how the vines had thrived in Châteauneuf-du-Pape.

Yet he felt no regret for the past, nor trepidation about the future.

55

When he was the Prince Imperial, Abdülaziz had felled an ox with a single blow exclaiming, "Like this I will destroy ignorance!" People had great expectations but, alas, the Sultan's idealism did not last. They said, "Sultan Mahmud had a passion for blood, Abdülmecid for women, for Abdülaziz it's gold."

It came upon him gradually after he had seen the splendors of Europe. He went on an unprecedented royal spending spree. He ordered dozens of pianos from England, which he had strapped on attendants' backs so that music could follow him wherever he walked. He ordered locomotives although there were no tracks on which to run them.

His palaces chirped and cackled with mechanical toys, clocks, and talking birds. One day he would be obsessed with collecting tigers, the next day giraffes. He would dispatch agents to India or Africa to acquire them. He enjoyed playing war with his real soldiers, going so far as to turn his palaces into battlegrounds.

When he met a civil servant named Aziz, he was enraged that anyone else should have his name and ordered all the men named Aziz to change theirs. He also rewrote the country's schoolbooks, deleting every Turkish defeat, the French Revolution, and any reference to Christianity.

Hardly a day passed when some new anecdote was not circulating about another explosion of wrath because the Minister of Finance refused to supply the money the Sultan demanded. All these eccentricities came to be exaggerated by the thousands of tongues in the court which slowly stretched the threads of conspiracy.

56

At the Tuileries, the Minister of the Interior solemnly handed Empress Eugénie the telegram, then discreetly left the room.

Eugénie read it with an empty expression on her face that seemed to stretch time itself, then burst into a scorching paroxysm of rage.

Her husband, Louis Napoléon III, Emperor of France, the grandnephew of Bonaparte, had been defeated in Sedan and had surrendered with eighty thousand men. He was being detained as a prisoner of war, at the Wilhelmshöhe Castle near Kassel.

At that moment, Eugénie's repressed anger over the Emperor's endless infidelities and all her other marital frustrations released themselves. She seemed to grow in size like a great actress at the peak moment of her performance.

There was no audience.

It was a moment of truth.

Not far away, in the City Hall, the New Republic was being reclaimed.

Outside the Tuileries, a large and noisy crowd accumulated. The railings were wrenched out, the gilded eagles on the imperial posts, the letter *N*, insignia of Napoléon and the Second Empire smashed to pieces. The mob shouted for her to leave.

On September 4, 1870, late morning, three deputies from the Legislative Corps visited the Empress at the Tuileries and urged her to abdicate.

"The sovereignty is not mine to dispense. I shall never abdicate," she replied.

Everyone fled the palace except a few of Eugénie's closest friends. But the Empress herself refused to move. "I'm not afraid of anything but falling into the hands of those animals who would surely defile my last hours with something disgraceful and grotesque," she confessed. She had heard them shout obscenities. She imagined them shaving her head, lifting her skirts, urinating on her. She saw bloody heads falling into a basket. Her morbid obsession with Marie Antoinette, whose bust she kept in her bedroom, reached its peak.

This, after all, was the same palace where Marie Antoinette had been forced to endure the Commune's hospitality after the storming of the Bastille. Eugénie imagined the unfortunate Queen scrutinized like an animal in a zoo until that fated August day when the bells rang in all the working-class neighborhoods and mobs stormed the Tuileries. The Swiss Guards had protected their Queen to the very end (would hers do the same?), but for naught. After looting the palace, the Communards had abandoned Marie Antoinette's quiet garden. But the eighteen naked statues stared blankly at a thousand corpses.

Toward dusk, out of moral exhaustion, Eugénie surrendered.

She left the Tuileries with nothing except her handbag, heavily veiled, a traveling cloak thrown over the black cashmere dress that she had not changed for days.

She took no money and no jewelry. From now on, she would have to rely on the kindness of strangers.

57

The smell of war was in the air. Everyone talked of the profit to be made. But Cassim Bey's faith rested in his vineyards. He mortgaged his land to expand them.

"One should never put at risk a gift from the Sultan," La Poupée told him. "It's sacrilege—almost as ominous as regicide."

How could she have prophesied the sequence of events?

Rumors had reached them that Eugénie and the dethroned Emperor were now living in exile in England, and that the Tuileries had been deserted. Cassim Bey thanked his lucky stars for having become a simple country gentleman, immune from all intrigue and blessed by his dream bride, who seemed to insulate him from all sophisticated forms of disaster.

But once again fate interfered. During the early spring, an unexpected hailstorm stripped the vines of their canopy. By the end of the season, Cassim Bey and La Poupée had lost their vineyards. The creditors claimed everything, leaving the couple only the old hunter's shack, surrounded by a land as wasted and barren as when they had first arrived.

58

On May 30, 1876, the Ottoman War Minister set off in a caïque across the Bosphorus to the white palace. With him he carried a *fetvah* from the Sheikh al-Islam, the supreme spiritual official of the Empire. This document authorized the Sultan's deposition on the grounds of "insanity and diversion of public revenue to private expenditure, and conduct generally injurious to state and community."

As the Minister landed on the marble waterfront, the wind was howling, the waves crashing on the steps. He had brought reinforcements. Two battalions on the land side and naval vessels on the Bosphorus side surrounded Dolmabahçe.

The Sultan lay in his enormous gilded bed with his seventeen-year-old Favorite, the beautiful Circassian named Mihri, as the first shots sounded from the gardens glistening with rain.

The Minister cleaved his way into the throne room to confront a crowd of hysterical eunuchs. As they squeaked and scurried, a figure in a pink nightshirt materialized at the top of the stairs. There was a dead silence.

The Sultan stood stock-still, then raised a sword above his head while his Favorite clung to him, sobbing in terror. Cautiously, the Minister approached with the decree and held it for him to read.

"Kismet," Abdülaziz sighed as he pushed it away.

At this moment, the Mother of the Veiled Heads, her hair tousled like a harpy's, ran down the stairs. She hurled herself at the Minister, clawing him in the face and flooring him with a kick to the stomach until the eunuchs pried them apart.

59

The guards escorted Abdülaziz to the Sublime Porte and locked him alone in the room where his uncle Selim III had once been brutally murdered.

The night was hell. The ghosts of the past Sultans haunted him until dawn.

The next day, they transferred him to a wing of the Çirağan Palace. Accompanying him were the Mother of the Veiled Heads and his Favorite, who was pregnant.

When Abdülaziz wandered into the garden of magnolias that he himself had planted, a guard ordered him to go inside. The humiliation increased the Sultan's distress. He remained awake for five days and five nights.

On June 3rd, he sat with his mother, watching the barges cross the Bosphorus. He was thinking of all the vessels that had floated across this ancient strait for eight thousand years, of all the emperors who had once ruled the city.

He stood up and looked at himself in a mirror. His own image terrified him.

"I need a pair of scissors to trim my beard," he told his mother. Then Abdülaziz asked to be left alone.

An hour later, the piercing screams of his Favorite rose up from an adjacent room. Through a window, she had seen the Sultan's head fall forward. By the time the door was forced open, it was too late. The portly figure of Abdülaziz lay on the floor, blood dripping from his wrists. The fatal scissors lay next to him on the floor.

Nineteen of the most prominent doctors in the city were summoned to establish the cause of the Sultan's death. They all confirmed it was suicide.

Not everyone agreed. There were whispers of assassination.

Dr. Milligen, an English physician, who nearly half a century earlier had attended Lord Byron in Missolonghi, asked the Mother of the Veiled Heads if she herself was in need of medical attendance.

"I am not in need of a doctor but an executioner, for I have murdered my son," she told him. "I was the one who gave him the scissors."

Within a few days, the Sultan's Favorite died in premature childbirth.

The child disappeared.

60

Cassim Bey and La Poupée lay side by side in bed in their small cabin. They yearned to join in the *rêve à deux* but sleep now weighed heavily, drifting their consciousness apart. In dark frustration, Cassim Bey was spawning a separate dream which La Poupée could neither enter nor undo. He dreamed that branches of alder, willow, and birch were strewn about their land covered with a great mountain of charcoal. And the sky was gunpowder black.

La Poupée watched him disconnect. She escaped into one of her own dreams in which their bed had caught on fire.

"Casimir," she called to him, using the secret name she still had for her husband. "Casimir, wake up, my love."

Flames surrounded them. The creditors had set fire to the already decapitated vineyards that Cassim Bey and La Poupée had lovingly tended for seasons, to make room for other crops.

Cassim Bey was no longer prosperous and La Poupée was expecting a child.

61

Cassim Bey traveled day and night on horseback by the sharp cliffs of the Babuna Mountains to the walled town of Skopje.

He asked for the Khazar's library where, it was rumored, there was a book that was a key to all books. A book in which one's whole life would be inscribed. For days, he searched and searched.

When at last Cassim Bey left the library some days later, raw from sitting, his weary eyes had a strange gleam of contentment. He had found the book of destiny which read, *Gunpowder.*

He heard strains of music coming from a *café chantant.* A young man, stretching his notes like Turkish taffy, was singing about Sultan Abdülaziz. He sang of his great palaces, his bevy of exotic birds, his exquisite women, his foolish pride, his madness, his suicide.

The singer continued with the melancholy refrain in the minor key:

> *But it was not his fault.*
> *It was his kismet.*
> *We are all slaves of fate.*
> *To which even the emperors are not immune.*
> *Great Sultan, rest in peace.*

Who could have foreseen their destiny on that magical dawn, Cassim Bey reflected, when the Sultan had encountered the Empress in the Beylerbey gardens? The scent of magnolia in the air, the dewy mist, the emerald pin.

"If *they* were not here, our ears would have witnessed a different verse on the Sultan's fate," a neighbor whispered, his eyes flicking toward the back of the room where lurked two men with scarlet fezzes—the insignia of the new Sultan's secret police.

62

The next day, Cassim Bey sold his horse in order to buy sulfur and saltpeter.

When he returned to Pirlepé, La Poupée watched as he mixed the two substances and heated the concoction in an iron pot. Then, he conducted the vapors to a cool chamber where flowers of sulfur rained like snowflakes. A phosphorous smell filled the air, wafting in a heavy gust of wind for miles.

Some people thought it smelled like war. Cassim Bey thought it smelled like gold.

That night in his bed with La Poupée next to him, he prayed for war. He repeated the same prayer for weeks and weeks.

La Poupée lay awake exhausted from weeping but unable to rest.

Cassim Bey continued to build cylinders out of iron and enclosed them in brick. For months he heated and cooled the powders until the consistency was so fine that it slipped through his fingers like flour.

Then, he ran to the village center where he filled the trophy cannon and fired it into the sky. The echo returned from the mountains and the locals ran into their houses, thinking the enemy had arrived.

Cassim Bey rolled in the pile of stones from the explosion and roared with laughter. "I've got it!"

As if they had heard his prayers, that spring the Serbs attacked the Albanians, the Croatians attacked the Macedonians, and the Bulgarians attacked the Greeks.

With each new conflict, the number of Cassim Bey's burning cylinders increased, as did the numbers of men he employed. The war devoured his gunpowder. The woods that once had smelled of frankincense, linden, and eucalyptus now exhaled a putrid sulfurous stench. A permanent black parasol formed over the stripped trees, their branches reaching up to the sky as if in prayer.

63

In no time, Cassim Bey repurchased his land and then many thousand acres surrounding it. He bought back his horse and other exotic breeds to fill his stables. For La Poupée, he purchased a splendid carriage. Dresses and jewels. And volumes of books. But even they could not comfort her soul.

"You make dust that destroys," she told Casimir.

"Wine or gunpowder, what difference does it make? Aren't both meant to intoxicate?"

"One is life, the other death."

"Perhaps they are one and the same."

The way one learns to ignore sounds that are constant and disturbing, they learned not to smell the air. And once again they learned to return to each other's dreams where everything was perfect. *Je vous aime.*

They had seven children one after another. Each one had a blue eye and a yellow one.

Up on the mountain, where the air was clean, Cassim Bey built a stone mansion with turrets. It was a replica of Grange du Souvenir, the château which had once been his home in Châteauneuf-du-Pape—where he had lived someone else's life.

Instead of grapes, the new family crest showed a cannon and smoke.

Cassim Bey was not the only one who prospered from the powder. The other landlords in the vicinity followed his style. Stone houses and châteaus sprouted everywhere. In no time, Pirlepé resembled a French province—except for the mosque which Cassim Bey had donated to the town, an edifice of midnight blue with crescents of gold and fleur-de-lis, where every day he went to pray.

64

In 1871 the Palace of Tuileries had been set on fire during another riot, then abandoned, left to disintegrate as if it were an Ozymandian curse on all rulers.

"There is not one little blackened stone here which is not to me a chapter in the bible of democracy," snickered Oscar Wilde.

The palace loomed, charred and disgraceful, for another decade until the decision came to demolish and create a public park. Some of the debris was auctioned off.

Among the buyers was a man dressed in a black skullcap and a furred robe. He had once personally designed the Empress's clothes and created her scent. Mr. Worth wandered through the rubble, picking up bits and pieces, each of which for him represented a particular moment, a story, and history.

From the salvaged parts, Worth created a garden of follies, which included Eugénie's bedroom windows, the ones she had copied from the Beylerbey. The windows which had once looked out to the Bosphorus, the Sublime Porte, and to passion.

65

On New Year's Day 1880, aboard a steam launch anchored at the mouth of the Rio Grande, Ferdinand de Lesseps's daughter Fernanda emptied the first shovel of sand into the champagebox. The Panama Canal had been initiated.

By the end of January 1881, the first group of French engineers of the Compagnie Universelle had arrived in Colón.

Eight years of valiant effort followed. The torrential rains, the oppression of humidity, and fatal disease took their toll.

The Panama Canal had not been as auspicious as the Suez. The piercing of the isthmus merely created a different kind of river, a river of conflict. In 1889, financial mismanagement, stock dysfunction, and negative publicity brought the work to a halt.

Lesseps returned to France consumed with doubt. In all his adventures, he had found neither love nor what he believed to be his true destiny. He felt he had simply been an instrument.

In the end, his epic vision had failed him.

66

Mr. Worth threw a party to celebrate his garden of follies.

In the crowd, Ferdinand de Lesseps noticed a mane of red hair he could not mistake. She was older now and retired from her profession, but with a substantial fortune to assure that she would live in style for the rest of her days.

Ferdinand de Lesseps gave her the letter that he still carried in his vest pocket.

She sipped the champagne with her small, voluptuous lips as she read.

Together, they witnessed the autumn leaves falling on the garden of follies to form a shroud over the remnants of the old Tuileries.

"What is hope, Monsieur de Lesseps?" she asked.

"Hope is agony postponed, my dear."

"Therefore, should one stop hoping?"

"The East was our greatest hope but it's too late. And I'm too old, and the West is moving too fast," Lesseps replied. "I think I'll make one last journey to the Orient. Would you care to accompany me?"

67

Lesseps's new mistress followed him. She was the former courtesan with the glorious red hair who had once lived above the arcades in the Palais Royal, the one with the voluptuous lips.

She was the one to sight the turrets of a château in the distance surrounded by farmhouses. The oddness of a French village with its mosque in the midst of the Macedonian wilderness intrigued the travelers.

Lesseps sent a messenger to the Manor with his calling card and a case of fine French wine.

The Lord of the Manor accepted the gift and invited the travelers to spend the night as his guests.

68

Inside, the château was not at all French.

The travelers found themselves, instead, in a setting of bright colors, of terra-cotta and tile, of priceless nomadic carpets. Of flowing fountains and singing birds. The air was scented with sweet flowers and spices, the divans covered with rich Ottoman fabrics, and golden tassels dangled from round cushions. Through skylights, light poured in and the dust sparkled with a golden sheen.

Wearing a turban on his head and a jeweled dagger on his side, Cassim Bey, dressed all in white, came to greet the guests. He resembled a magician.

The thrill of coincidence agitated the air as the eyes of the two men met. They had not seen each other since

Compiègne, the night of the banquet when the Empress Eugénie had lured Casimir de Châteauneuf to his fate.

And next to Lesseps stood the woman who had once been Casimir's mistress.

"How did you become all this?" Lesseps asked.

"The frailties of human passion. The same as we all do."

"We all have our share in it, I suppose."

In the kitchen the cooks prepared the delicacies of the region—from the ingredients that La Poupée had cultivated in a garden distant from the sulfurous air. The hunting and mushroom season had arrived with bounty. The chestnuts had burst out of their husks. But the vineyards still remained barren.

Cassim Bey opened a bottle of wine from the case that was Lesseps's gift. He sniffed the cork, poured a little in a glass, then swished it around in his mouth. He took in the scent, then a slow, long sip into the back of his throat. He swallowed. His eyes burned and he made a sound of great satisfaction of which only a Frenchman is capable.

He had recognized immediately the exceptional and unique taste of Châteauneuf-du-Pape. The label read: *Grange du Souvenir*. The proprietors, André, Antoine, and Alphonse de Châteauneuf.

The mistress remembered when she had sat in this

same configuration, between these same two men at Compiègne before they were to leave for Suez, each to unite with his Orient. She asked for another glass of wine.

"Love is the name given to sorrow to console those who suffer. Remember?" she asked Cassim Bey. "We suffer because we either desire what we have not or possess what we no longer desire."

"I remember. But suffering is not your ailment, I hope, Madam?"

"No. I am reconciled to the eternal isolation in which my heart remains entombed. It must be my fate, Casimir."

At that moment, La Poupée raised her veil. The two women's eyes met. The mistress held her breath. The wife had one blue eye and a yellow one. She was the face in the tiny painting, the one Casimir had bought at that Orientalia shop one autumn afternoon at the Palais Royal. The face that had inspired him to love her in such a way that night that she had never forgotten. The face that had lured him to another continent. The face that had caused him to erase his identity. The face of a doll.

"What happens if we possess what we once desired?" the mistress asked her former lover.

"It brings us closer to our destiny. We become human."

"And if we cannot?"

"Then we belong only in the realm of the senses."

"Which is better?"

"That depends on one's fate."

"Are you suggesting then that fate and love are one and the same?"

At this instant, La Poupée spoke for the first time. "Not the same but one always invites the other, Madame. And it is never what we expect. But the search keeps us thriving. Otherwise, we would perish."

Her peculiar eyes were hypnotic. The rest of the night, the guests allowed themselves to be transported to the continent of her reveries. They listened as La Poupée's sonorous voice, her whimsical Martinique French evoked smiles and tears by turns.

69

The following morning the visitors departed.

Lesseps told Cassim Bey that he could return to France with them, if he wished. They had diplomatic clearance, they could easily conceal his identity and smuggle him out of this foreign land.

Casimir laughed. "The inescapable chain of events has brought me to this point, it is not I who have caused these things to happen, Ferdinand. One has no need to return to the past or seek one's future when one meets one's destiny. I'm a fortunate man because mine has found me."

He gazed at La Poupée sitting by a fountain, surrounded by their children. They were all listening to her story with dreamy concentration. All with one blue eye, one yellow.

Far in the distance, smoke was rising from the mountain and the thunderous sounds of cannons made the earth tremble.

The smoke of gunpowder was in the air.

Acknowledgments

I thank the madness of the Frenchman who embraced passion as his fate and the woman who could inspire him so. I'm grateful to my grandmother, Zehra, for spinning their story which fired my child's imagination and grew into dreams for so many years.

I thank the stars for being born in a city of such superb poetry so that I could imagine an impossibly romantic setting. To another madman of such stubborn determination, whom I met years later, whose character merged with the story in those dreams.

I thank my wonderful agent Bonnie Nadell, who rose me out of melancholy and who steered these pages, nine months pregnant, through the labyrinths of publishers. Robin Desser, who gave me the incentive to push through a diaphanous fog. Leslie Schnur, who grasped the vision. Kathleen Jayes, my editor, whose tenacious intelligence guided it through.

To Fred Hill, Irene Moore, Caroline Sincerbeaux, Isabel Allende, Diane Johnson, Noelle Oxenhandler, Fatima Mernissi, Katherine Neville, Terence Clarke, Stephen Huyler, Paul Fournel, Evelyne and Jeffrey Thomas, Nurshen Bakir, Lydia Titcomb, my cyberspace complice, and to Vicky Doubleday, who took it to the other world, a thousand and one kisses.

Thanks to all the production, design, sales, and promotion

people and the reviewers and the booksellers whom I have not yet met since this part of the book always precedes their great contribution and one regrets later for not having known them. And to all the readers who, in the duration of these pages, will become my intimate friends.

And finally, to Robert, who wrote me love notes every morning and made my coffee.

About the Author

ALEV CROUTIER was born in Turkey. She has written and directed award-winning independent films and was awarded a Guggenheim Fellowship (the first ever for a screenplay) for her work on *Tell Me a Riddle*. She is the author of the internationally acclaimed bestseller *Harem: The World Behind the Veil*. She divides her time between San Francisco and Paris.